BLADE

CUTTING LOOSE

Blade has done all he can—shaken up the city, turned the gangster bosses against Hawk, his most dangerous enemy, and given the police the information they need to destroy the man for ever.

But Hawk is still free, still powerful, and more angry than ever. He has men swarming over the city in search of the boy who has betrayed him. Blade can take no more. All he wants is to cut loose, give up his past, make a clean break. It should be possible.

But then they catch him.

The seventh title in this ground-breaking series from Tim Bowler, the Carnegie Medal-winning author of *River Boy*, *Starseeker*, *Frozen Fire* and *Bloodchild*. Blade is finished, but his enemy is just getting started . . .

Tim Bowler

tim bowler
winner of the carnegie medal

BLADE
CUTTING LOOSE

7

book

OXFORD
UNIVERSITY PRESS

OXFORD
UNIVERSITY PRESS

Great Clarendon Street, Oxford OX2 6DP

Oxford University Press is a department of the University of Oxford.
It furthers the University's objective of excellence in research, scholarship,
and education by publishing worldwide in

Oxford   New York

Auckland   Cape Town   Dar es Salaam   Hong Kong   Karachi
Kuala Lumpur   Madrid   Melbourne   Mexico City   Nairobi
New Delhi   Shanghai   Taipei   Toronto

With offices in

Argentina   Austria   Brazil   Chile   Czech Republic   France   Greece
Guatemala   Hungary   Italy   Japan   Poland   Portugal   Singapore
South Korea   Switzerland   Thailand   Turkey   Ukraine   Vietnam

Oxford is a registered trade mark of Oxford University Press
in the UK and in certain other countries

British Library Cataloguing in Publication Data

Data available

ISBN: 978-0-19-275600-8

1 3 5 7 9 10 8 6 4 2

Printed in Great Britain

Paper used in the production of this book is a natural,
recyclable product made from wood grown in sustainable forests.
The manufacturing process conforms to the environmental
regulations of the country of origin.

For Rachel
with my love

The bridge slips from my grasp. I peer down at the river. It's yawning in the night, far below me, and I'm falling towards it like a wingless bird. Dead in my body, dead in my heart. Ready to die again.

Only I can't.

A weightless moment, an ecstasy of fear, then the vice closes round me, hooks my chest, jerks me upwards. Something hard slams into my back. The metal rails at the top of the bridge. My feet slither back on the ledge, skid off again.

1

The vice tightens, hauls me back against the top of the bridge. I hang there, whimpering, kicking my legs. Ruby's voice blares down at me.

'Chicken bastard!'

She's got me from behind. Must have reached through the rails just as I let go of 'em. Got both her arms under mine and they're locked round my chest. And now she's yanking me back towards the ledge.

'Chicken waster,' she mutters, 'chicken bloody—'

'Ruby—'

'Think killing yourself's going to sort everything?'

'Ruby—'

'Going to pay your debt to my daughter?'

'Ruby—'

'Well, it ain't! Cos jumping off a bridge don't pay no debt to Becky! Don't pay no debt to nobody!'

'Ruby!' I splutter. 'Ruby!'

She takes no notice, just goes on hauling me up.

'Let me go!' I scream.

'Don't tempt me.'

'I'm a piece of shit!'

'Yeah, like I don't know that.'

I kick my legs again, try to wriggle free. I don't

want to live, Bigeyes. I don't deserve to. Becky died in the river. And she died cos of me. So I got to die there too. No question. I got to die there too.

I stare down at Mother Grime. Her black watery mouth's still open, waiting for me. I wriggle again, thrash about. Makes no difference. Ruby only tightens her grip, goes on pulling. I feel my feet clock back on the ledge. Ruby crabs her arms round my stomach, snags me hard against the rails.

I feel my hands close round the metal. Like they want to.

Even if I don't.

I shut my eyes. No sounds from the bridge. No voices, no traffic. Just me and Ruby breathing hard, the river whispering below. Then Ruby's voice again, still raging.

'Think killing yourself's going to put you right, huh?'

I don't answer.

'Huh?' she snaps.

I open my eyes, stare down again. Mother Grime goes on flowing. I think of Becky's body, swallowed by water. How the grinks in the van shot her all those years ago, heaved her off the bridge to disappear for ever.

How it was my fault. Cos they were my enemies, Bigeyes, not hers. But she died and I lived. It's not right. Becky was my friend. My best friend ever. I should be with her, right now. Whatever her mum says.

Ruby tightens her grip, like she's picked up my thought.

'Still want to jump, right?' she fumes.

I say nothing. She leans her head close to the rails.

'Yeah, you do. You want to jump. You know why? Cos you're a coward. A slimy little coward. You think jumping off wipes your slate clean. Well, it don't. It's just the chicken way out. But I guess that's cool with you. The chicken way out. Cos it don't take no guts, huh? No responsibility, no—'

'Ruby—'

'Go and jump!' she bellows. 'If that's all you got. Cos I'm telling you—if that's the best you got for Becky, then you ain't worth piss. You want to top yourself? Go ahead!'

She lets go, slips her arms free.

'Or do something better. Your call.'

Sound of footsteps on the bridge. Ruby tramping away, heading for the north side. I watch her for a moment through the rails. She doesn't look back, not once. I want her to. But I know she won't. She'll just go on walking.

If I jump, she won't even notice.

I stare down at the river again.

'Mother Grime,' I murmur. 'You bitch.'

Look back at Ruby. She's disappeared from view, but she'll still be walking.

Still not looking.

'Bitch,' I murmur after her. 'Yeah, Ruby, you too.'

I climb back over the rail, drop down onto the bridge. Ruby's close to the north side now, trigging steadily on. I start to walk after her. Don't ask me why, Bigeyes, cos I don't know. She's the last person in the world I want right now.

And I'm the last person she wants.

But I keep walking, walking, walking.

Then I catch it. The sound of the motor. Coming from the south side. Doesn't sound like a problem.

Shouldn't even be worried about it. Middle of the night, quiet time, but there's been other traffic, a bit anyway. This could be anyone.

Only it's not, Bigeyes. It's not anyone. It's trouble.

Don't ask me how I know.

I don't even need to look round. But I do. And it's what I thought. A van chunking over the bridge towards me, towards Ruby. Just like it did the day Becky got shot. And now here's her mum in just the same danger.

And once again—cos of me.

I scream at Ruby.

'Run for it! Run for it!'

I race down towards her. She's not running but she's turned and she's watching me hare across the bridge.

'Ruby! Run!'

She's still not running. She's stopped and she's just watching me. What's wrong with her? She must have seen the van steaming up behind me. There'll be grinks in it, just like there were with Becky. It's all happening again, like it did three years ago.

Sound of a shot.

Misses me, misses Ruby, but now she starts running, only—Jesus!—she's cutting the wrong way. Meant to be blasting off the north side but she's belting straight at me.

'Ruby, go back! Head for the alleyways! Other side of the main road!'

Engine's getting louder. Glance round. Van's close to the middle of the bridge now. Three gobbos in the front, one leaning out the window. Another shot.

Misses again.

I stumble on and here's Ruby bustling up.

'Ruby, for Christ's sake—'

She doesn't answer, just grabs my hand, pulls me over to the other side of the bridge. Van swerves across the road towards us. I'm praying for something else to slum up. Car, bus, taxi, whatever. But still nothing.

Van skews to a halt. Two of the gobbos pile out.

Ruby's still pulling me towards the edge of the bridge, and now I see where she's heading. The steps down to the wharf.

'Not down there, Ruby.'

She takes no notice, just goes on pulling.

'Ruby!'

She tugs me harder.

'OK, OK,' I mutter. 'I got what you want.'

She lets go and we pile down the steps. Feet pound behind us on the bridge.

This is a dronky idea, Bigeyes. I should never have let Ruby jam us down here. We'll never get away. The grinks are too fast, too strong, and they'll block the way back. And they got guns.

Shit!

First I get Becky killed, now it's going to be her mum. And Ruby was only trying to clip me clear of these grinks. I got to do my best for her. For Becky's sake too. Sound of feet above us.

Thump, thump, thump.

They're taking the steps in twos and threes. We got a lead but not much.

'Faster,' says Ruby.

Bottom of the steps and here's the wharf. Dimpy place to hide. We're separated from the bank by a small channel, got nothing to the left and just a short quay to the right with a few slaggy river boats and a big old motor cruiser at the end. No lights on any of 'em.

But we're not here to hide. I worked out Ruby's plan on the way down. She thought the alleyways up top are too far to get to, since the gobbos have got guns. So she's led 'em down here and now we got to belt back to the street, taking the steps up the other side of the bridge.

And lose the bastards on the way.

There's just a chance it might work. Both the gobbos are on this set of steps. I can tell from the sound of 'em. We might just be able to wig it up the others. I start to cut right but Ruby catches my arm.

Jesus, Bigeyes. Now what?

She's staring at the boats, and now she's pulling me off to the left. I glare at her. Heavy breaths above us, feet getting louder. Ruby glares back, pulls me harder, and now I get it. She's not heading for the other steps. She's slipping us round the back of these ones.

Another crap idea. Even worse than coming down in the first place. But we got no time to do anything else now. The grinks are almost down. I let her pull me round the base of the steps. She draws me in close to her, arm over my shoulder. I feel her breathing hard, her body warm against me.

Not acting like she's scared.

I'm telling you, Bigeyes, she's something, this woman. Might have made a dimpy choice coming down here but she's something. No wonder Becky had so much bottle. She got it from her mum.

Thump, thump.

Silence.

The grinks have hit the wharf. Only they're not moving. They're standing there, just hidden, other side of the steps. I glance at Ruby. She's pulled out her mobile.

Got one arm holding me close, and we're crouching in the darkness with those two grinks still standing there on the other side of the steps, and with her other hand she's texting.

Catches my eye, looks down again, goes on texting, sparks off a message, slips the mobile back in her pocket. Cool as a breeze. Not like me. I'm starting to breathe blood.

I can feel it pounding in my head. I got my hands moving inside my coat and they're squeezing the knives, just like they used to. Only it's not the same, not now. Cos I don't love the blades any more. I hate 'em. But it makes no difference.

My hands still find 'em.

Hold 'em tight. They're ready. Won't do much good probably. Least one of these grinks has got a gun. Maybe both of 'em. Maybe all three. But they haven't found us yet so we still got surprise on our side.

And that means a chance.

Ruby looks at me sharp. I try to read her face in the darkness. It's saying something, something I can't make out. And then I catch it. Something I recognize from the past. Cos it's something Becky used to have in her face.

The word no.

In her face, in her eyes.

No.

That's all.

No to what? Don't play thick, Bigeyes. No to everything. That's what it meant. Everything that's wrong, she meant. And there was plenty wrong back then.

11

You bet there was. Right now it's the knives that's wrong.

Yeah, even here, with grinks ready to wipe us out, Ruby's felt my hands move inside my coat and she's guessed what they got, and her face is saying that word again, throwing it at me through the darkness.

No.

I feel my fingers ease.

Just a bit.

Sound of movement, other side of the steps. Slow, slow. They're not moving away. They're checking round and they're taking their time. They know we're still down here. They'd have rushed up the other steps by now if they thought we'd blasted out that way.

So much for Ruby's plan.

They'll check everywhere, including here.

And they're not stupid. One of 'em'll keep close to the steps. See what I mean? Shadow moving over to the right. Ruby's clapped it too. Pulls me closer to her, crouching even lower. Shadow hasn't turned, hasn't seen us yet. It's wandering down the wharf, stopping by each of the river boats, peering down.

And the other grink?

You guessed it. Bastard's still standing at the bottom of the steps. There's no way he's going to let us back up again. Easy piss. He stands here, guards these steps, keeps an eye on the other ones at the same time. Second gobbo goes looking.

Third gobbo up on the bridge checks down too. I'm guessing he can't see too good from up there, what with the bridge in the way, so we may just stay cute from him, but he's another problem we got to smack.

Shadow's stopped. Halfway down the wharf. Fixing one of the river boats. It's rocking in the swell. Sound of a cough from his mate. Still standing close to the bottom of the steps, just the other side of the brick. Check out the shadow again.

It's moving. Guy's clambering aboard the boat. Disappears from view round the back of the cabin. Only now Ruby's shifting too. Got a hand over my mouth.

Yeah, right. Like I'm going to suddenly blab a noise. Like I haven't spent my whole life ducking slime. I shake my head, scowl at her. She takes her hand away, grips my arm, edges me towards the side of the wharf.

Christ, no.

Effing water, just below us. I feel the old fear flick over me. Can't stop it. Ruby takes no notice. Maybe she doesn't realize, just thinks I'm freaking about the gobbos. Well, I am. I know what they can do, more than she does, maybe, but it's the water that's choking my head.

She's stopped again, still holding my arm, and now she's checking behind. I don't need to. I've checked already. First gobbo's still hidden behind the steps, other one's still on the boat. But we've moved out of the darkness and we're right at the edge of the wharf.

Moment the guy on the boat climbs back to the quay, he'll see us crouching here. I grab Ruby, try to push her back towards the steps. But she won't go. And now she's forcing me even closer to the water. Then I see it.

The ladder down the side of the wharf.

Into the river.

No boat, nothing. Just Mother Grime, licking her

lips. There's waves punching up against the wall. I shudder, check the ladder again. It's oily and covered in weed. I feel Ruby steer me towards it. I look round, catch her eyes.

Urging me.

Check the wharf. Shadow's appeared again, climbing back onto the quay. Hasn't looked this way yet. Could do any moment. Don't, you bastard. Go the other way. Check the other boats.

He doesn't. Just stands there, staring towards the other steps. He could look back any moment. His mate's still here. He's bound to check round. And then he'll see us. Ruby squeezes my arm again. And this time I move.

Over the edge of the wharf, grip the ladder. Metal's cold and wet and I hate the smell of the river hissing up at me. Clamber down, slow as I can, but not too slow cos Ruby's got to get down too, and she's got to be quick.

But here she is, climbing after me, quiet and sharp, like she's done this all her life. Stops just above me, looks down, nods me towards the river. Jesus, Bigeyes. I don't want to go any closer.

She nods again.

I try to control my hands. They're shaking bad now, and so's the rest of my body. Yeah, I know. I wanted to jump into Mother Grime earlier. But that was off the bridge.

I thought I'd die straight off from the impact, and if not that, then I reckoned I'd be so stunned I'd drown first gulp. But this is different. The water's over my feet now and it's creeping like blood.

Then I catch a new sound. Feet clumping down from the bridge. And voices. Only not from the steps but from the wharf. And it's not the two grinks. It's women. One of 'em bawls out.

'Who the hell are you?'

Raspy voice. Sounds like a hard shibo. I cling to the ladder rail, catch Ruby peering up at the top of the wharf, listening, like me. Second woman, another shibo. Tough, spitty.

'You looking for trouble?'

Third woman, same again. Mocking too.

'Cos if you're looking for fun, boys, you ain't getting none 'ere.'

Footsteps getting louder. And this isn't women. It's

gobbos. Least three. Don't ask me how I know. They're muttering as they come. Hard slugs, same as the women. Now a new sound.

Running.

No prizes for guessing what that is. The grink by the stairs is wigging it. He's seen what's coming down and he's blasting off towards the other way out. His mate'll be doing the same. Yeah, he is. Listen to the women.

'Not stopping, then, boys?'

'Come on!'

'Show us what you got!'

I know what they got, Bigeyes. They got guns. So those shibos better watch their mouths. But it should be OK. The grinks won't use 'em down here, not for no reason. They'll pull 'em out if the shibos and these other gobbos get too close, but they're not looking for trouble.

They're looking for me. So as long as no one gets in their way, they'll keep the guns for later. More shouts from the shibos.

'Go on, boys!'

'Piss off!'

'Bastards!'

Sound of running up the other steps. Crane my head up. We're right under the bridge here and no one can see the ladder from up top. Don't think so anyway. Hidden from the road too, cos of the angle. So there's no way the grinks can shoot down at us, even if they know where we are.

But we're not out of danger.

No way.

I got these new dronks to think about. And the grinks won't go far either. They'll hang around nearby, wait for these nebs to go, then come back. They didn't see Ruby and me slam out, so they'll guess we're still down here.

Sound of an engine up above. The van, taking off.

Don't be fooled, Bigeyes. It's like I said. They won't be going far. They'll keep the top of the steps in view. So we're still in the grime. Ruby twists her body, leans closer.

'Now listen good,' she mutters. 'You wait here. On this ladder. You don't move, right? You stay here till someone come for you.'

'What you going to do?'

'Talk to my friends.'

I stare up into her face.

'Those guys up there,' I say. 'The ones just came down. You texted 'em, right?'

She shakes her head.

'I texted the women. They work on that old motor cruiser at the end of the wharf.'

'Work?'

'Yeah.' She fixes me hard. 'Work.'

Silence. Just the ripple of Mother Grime over the base of the ladder.

'Wait here,' says Ruby.

She starts to climb up the ladder.

'Thanks,' I call after her.

'Wait till someone come.'

And she's over the top and gone.

More silence, then a burst of voices from the gobbos.

'Hey, Rubes!'

'What's going on, babe?'

'You hittin' some shit?'

I cling to the ladder, listen. The shibos have joined the group too and Ruby's talking. But she's speaking low and I can't catch what she's saying. All I know is she's talking and they're listening. Like I told you, Bigeyes, she's something, that woman.

And I'll tell you something else. She's smart too. Cos listen—I just worked it out. She took one look at the alleyways off the bridge, knew we wouldn't make 'em, so she hit the steps.

First plan, I'm guessing. Lead 'em down here and lose 'em on the way up the other steps. But that was never going to work, cos the grinks came down too quick. Moment we hit the wharf I knew that. And Ruby knew it too.

But she had a second plan. Even as we were standing there, she was checking the old boat. Knew the shibos might be there, and maybe some other help. But there were no lights on. So she was cool enough to think of a third plan.

She knew that racing for the cruiser and taking a chance was a dimpy idea. If we found no nebs on board, we'd be trapped straight up. The grinks would have us on the boat and no way off. So she pulls me out of sight, texts the shibos, tells 'em to ring their mates and get 'em here quick.

Then thinks up Plan Number Four.

Slinks the two of us down the ladder. Case the help doesn't show and we got to blind it on our own. Some woman. Trouble is, thinking of Ruby makes me think of Becky again. I look down at the black water.

Feel the tears try to come.

Then realize the voices have vanished from the wharf. They're up on the far steps, moving higher, and now they're up on the bridge, and now . . .

They're gone.

I grip the metal rung. I'm starting to shiver. Mother Grime's slopping over my shoes and trouser bottoms. I spit down into her face, spit again, growl at her, climb up another two rungs, stop.

Ruby said to wait. I don't want to. I want to scramble up onto the quay and run my legs off. Before the grinks come back. But Ruby said to wait. So I got to stay put. I owe her that. Even though it seems like another bad idea.

Then I see a face looking down from the wharf.

Woman, about twenty-five. Black hair, zip eyes. Piercings all over—lips, nose, ears, brows. Christ knows what else she's got. No question who she is. One of the shibos from the motor cruiser.

She looks me over like I'm scum, then calls down to me. I recognize the voice. She was the one who taunted the grinks loudest.

'Let's go,' she snarls.

I climb up, punch a look round. No sign of any other nebs. Just me and the shibo standing here. I check her over.

Not wearing much but she's dramatic. Skimpy piece of nothing on top, even less underneath, but it's all black and leather, and there's bling bouncing every time she moves. Neck, wrists, ankles, fingers. Tats down her arms and round her middle. Snakes mostly.

She gives me a smile. It's like a winter's night. I cop a glint of more bling on her teeth and tongue. Then I realize it's not a smile. She's just opened her mouth to say something.

'Come with me.'

And that's it.

Turns and heads towards the old motor cruiser.

Or rather strides. Got some clash, this shibo, and too much spit for my liking. But I'm more freaked by the grinks. Like I told you, they won't have gone. And what's worse—they'll be ringing for backup.

Shibo goes on striding towards the boat. I follow, checking every way I can. Can't see any danger. Just the river boats rocking and Mother Grime licking past the wharf, and up above, the underside of Bogeybum Bridge. And up above that, a speckle of stars.

Shibo stops by the cruiser, fixes me.

'Get in the boat.'

I feel a shiver. Yeah, Bigeyes. You know about me and boats. And effing water. But I guess there's no other way. I start to climb onto the motor cruiser. Shibo clicks her tongue.

'Not that boat.'

She nods towards the stern.

'The dinghy.'

I check down towards it. Little shadow, bobbing on a line. Jesus, I hate these things. Even smaller than the one Bex put me in that time. And the water's more chippy than it was then. Don't shake your head, Bigeyes.

It is.

Look at those waves.

'Get in the dinghy,' snaps the shibo.

I trig down the quay, stop at the dinghy. Dronky thing. Looks like it wants to sink all by itself. I wish it bloody would. Oars already in it, and the rowlock things, or whatever they're called. I take a breath, sit down on the edge of the quay. Got to be a way into this dimpy thing.

Can't jump.

'Use the ladder,' calls the shibo.

She's still standing by the middle of the cruiser. Can't work out why she hasn't come down too. I check the quayside again. Yeah, she's right. More oily little rungs down the side of the wharf into the water.

I glance at her again.

Still not moving. Don't feel good about this, Bigeyes. First the water, now this woman trashing my head. She makes a huffy noise. I climb down the ladder, fumble into the dinghy. Look round. Shibo goes on watching me for a bit, then reaches out to the cruiser, knocks the side of the cabin with her fist.

Sound of movement inside, then a gobbo sticks his

head out of a hatchway. Can't see his face but he's got dreads. About the same age as the shibo, I'm guessing. She leans close, mutters something. He twists round in the hatchway, checks me out, looks back at the shibo.

More muttering.

Now the shibo's coming over. Moves quick, confident. Down the ladder, into the dinghy, nods me towards the stern. I shift down there. She sits on the thwart, casts off, grabs the oars. Dinghy wallows. I clutch the side, feel my mind spin.

Shibo takes no notice, just eases us past the motor cruiser. But we're not heading out into Mother Grime. We're slipping in towards the wall, right under Bogeybum Bridge. And now we're creeping along it, down the narrow channel between the wharf and the bank.

I give the shibo a look.

'What we going this way for?'

'Was I talking to you?'

She's got a voice like a whip.

'Just asking,' I mutter.

She rows on, right under the bridge and close to the wall. Here's the ladder me and Ruby hung from. Looks spooky from the water, but not as spooky as the water itself. I'm dreading what's coming when we head out into the river.

But we're not doing that either.

We've stopped by the steps I came down with Ruby and we're sitting here in the darkness, oars dripping. I want to ask the shibo what she's waiting for, but there's no point. Her eyes tell me to keep quiet. So I keep quiet, and wait, still clutching the side of the dinghy.

Then I hear it.

The chug of the engine. Shibo looks back down the wharf and I do the same. The old cruiser's setting off. Two figures on her. The gobbo I saw earlier, now at the wheel, and a second gobbo, coiling rope.

No lights on still.

Just a ghostly shape, purring out into the river. Straight out, too, towards the south side, tracking the course of the bridge. I glance at the shibo. She cracks her eyes at me, like she doesn't like me looking at her, then dips her oars, and we're moving again.

Out from under the bridge, and now we can be seen from above. The shibo looks up and I do too, searching for grinks. Figures up on the bridge but it's hard to make 'em out in the darkness. No sign of Ruby.

One of 'em gives a nod.

Just a small movement but I catch it in the night. It's not to me. It's to the shibo. I can tell. Some kind of signal. Don't ask me what it means. Or the motor cruiser cutting off to the other side of Mother Grime.

The shibo rows on, along the line of the wall. There's a swell now, rolling across from the centre of the river and washing up the bank. Swish, swish, and back towards the boat. Makes me choke in my head. I'm squeezing the side of the boat and I'm trembling bad.

The shibo looks me over.

'What's up with you?' she goes.

'Nothing.'

'You're shaking.'

'I don't like water.'

'You scared of it?'

'No.'

'You is.'

She rows on, frowning. I check the wall. No faces looking down from the top, no sight of the road. I check the river again. Can't see the motor cruiser, but I can hear it. Sounds like it's a good way over the other side of Mother Grime.

I don't like this, Bigeyes. I was starting to trust Ruby. I mean, she got me off the bridge and away from the grinks. But into what? I don't like this shibo and I don't like the look of her mates.

We're moving closer to the wall. I check it over again. Maybe the shibo's just keeping us in the shadow. But I'm guessing it's more than that. Yeah, it is. See that? Steps cut into the wall. Shibo rows up to 'em.

'Get out,' she says.

I check over the side of the dinghy. Water's swirling over the steps, sucking in, sucking out. No way I'm putting my feet there.

'Get on with it,' mutters the shibo.

Yeah, like it's a whack getting out.

'Get on with it!' she goes.

I bung a scowl at her. Makes no difference. She just jerks her head at the steps. I climb over the side of the boat, gripping tight as I can. The water goes on churning round the brick.

I plant a foot on one of the steps, slip, gasp, catch my footing again, clutch the boat. I'm half-in, half-out, and the dinghy's pulling away from the wall.

'Christ's sake,' splutters the shibo.

Chugs her oars, eases the boat closer again.

'Now get out!'

I slither over onto the steps, fumble for something to hold. Feel a wave thump over my legs, crab me off balance. I start to tumble, flap my arms about.

'The rail!' shouts the woman.

I see it, grab it, squeeze it. I'm breathing hard, shaking worse than ever. I take a moment, look up. The steps lead all the way to the road. I take some more breaths, check round.

Shibo's already pulling back towards the wharf. Catches my eye, glares, rows on. I turn back to the steps, make my way slowly up. I got a bad feeling about this, Bigeyes. And I'm not talking about the water. I'm talking about what's waiting for me up top.

I want to pretend the shibo was just doing Ruby a favour. Getting me off the wharf and back to the road so I can wig it by myself. I want to pretend that was the plan all along. But it's not going to be that simple.

Don't ask me how I know.

I go on climbing, climbing, climbing. Yeah, like I thought. Here's the top of the steps. Here's the road. And here's the van.

Waiting for me.

Only I'm wrong. It's waiting for me, yeah, but it's not the van. It's another van. Same colour, same type. But another van. Dirtier than the other one. Black gobbo standing outside it. About thirty. Hard dronk. No bling. Just muscle.

Doesn't like me. That's bung-clear.

But I don't like him much either.

'Get in the back,' he booms.

I don't. I'm checking the road. Bogeybum Bridge is off to the left, half-hidden by the bend in the road. Nothing to the right, apart from taxis rolling. No sign of grinks either way. But they can't be far. I look back at the gobbo.

No way I'm getting in the van with him.

He glowers.

'Ruby said get in the back.'

'She in there too?'

'No.'

'Then why should I get in the back?'

He says nothing. Just goes on glowering.

'You helped me,' I say. 'You and your mates. So thanks. But I'll take it from here.'

He pulls out a gun, points it at me.

'Get in the back.'

'That Ruby talking?'

'No,' he growls. 'That me talking.'

I get in. Nothing else to do. Two shibos in the back of the van. Black janxes, about Ruby's age. They just stare. Gobbo slams the door, walks round, climbs into the driver's seat. Nobody else with him in the front of the van. Turns round, stabs me with his eyes.

'You stay there,' he grunts. 'You got that?'

I fix him back.

'What else am I going to do, claphead? You got a gun.'

Gobbo narrows his eyes.

Shit, Bigeyes. I shouldn't have said that. What was

I thinking of? He watches me, stretches out his arm, points the gun at my heart. I stiffen. Part of me wants to squirm backwards. Rest of me doesn't want to flinch.

I keep still, somehow. No point moving anyway. Nowhere to hide in here. Close by I feel the women watching. He gives a smile, squeezes the trigger—then pulls.

Gun gives a click.

Nothing more.

The shibos laugh. Gobbo does the same, a great bellow. Then throws the gun towards me. It slides along the floor of the van, thumps up against my leg. I don't pick it up, just stare back at the gobbo. He gives me a sneer, turns, starts the engine. And we set off down the road.

Towards Bogeybum Bridge.

Yeah, Bigeyes, now I'm confused. Can't work out what these nebs want. They're something to do with Ruby but that's all I know. They haven't hurt me yet and they've probably rescued me from the grinks. For the moment anyway.

But they don't like me.

Not one bit.

It's not just that shibo in the rowing boat. The gobbo in the front thinks I'm a dungpot. I can tell from his manner. And these two janxes in the back are staring at me like that shibo in the boat did.

Like I'm scum.

But maybe that's it, Bigeyes. Maybe I am scum.

Ruby should have let me jump. Do something better, she said. Yeah, but what? I've done all I can. Shunted Hawk with the gangster bojos. Given Bannerman all the bung about Hawk, told him where the stuff is, specially the backup hard drive from Hawk's computer. That's the thing he's got to do.

He's got to lift that backup drive.

It could finish Hawk. Might be the only thing that can.

So what else?

Eh? For a piece of scum.

What else but die?

Do something better. Yeah, Ruby. But what?

We're turning in the road, heading away from Bogeybum Bridge.

Thank Christ for that. But I'm still scared, Bigeyes.

Cos I still don't know who these nebs are or what they want. One of the shibos speaks.

'You're the shit that got Becky killed.'

So that's it. They know about Becky. Ruby must have told 'em, before she blasted off wherever she's gone. No wonder they hate me. But what does it mean? They've got me away from the grinks, and Ruby must have fixed that. But what do they want? And what does she want?

I offered her my life.

And that wasn't good enough.

So what else can I give her?

The shibos are still watching me. The one who spoke leans closer.

'You're the shit that got Becky killed.'

'You just said that.'

'I'm saying it again.'

Her mate stuffs a glare on me.

I stuff one back. I hate these janxes. I know they're right about Becky. And they're right about me. I am a shit. But it doesn't mean I got to be polite. Cos they certainly won't be.

Van rumbles on through the night. I can tell which

way we're going without looking. Same as in the old city. I know my way too good round here to get lost. Even stuck inside a van.

But I can see anyway, through the windscreen. We've cut round Bogeybum Bridge, given it plenty of room, but now we're cracking towards Mother Grime again. I'm guessing the gobbo's taking us to the south side.

Told you.

We're clattering over the next bridge down from Bogeybum. Old Smokey. That's what I call this one. Always have done. Don't ask me why. I go on staring out through the windscreen. Sky's lightening, see? Just a bit. But what kind of a dawn will it be? And how many times have I wondered that?

I'll tell you, Bigeyes. Lots of times.

That's the crack of it. Dawn after dawn after bloody dawn. I'm fourteen, Bigeyes, and I've seen more dawns than I deserve to already. And every time I see one, I ask myself if it's going to be the last.

We're over Old Smokey now and hammering off south of the river.

I lean back against the side of the van, fix my eyes

on the janxes. They're leaning together, murmuring stuff I can't hear. Rough women. Not as sparky as the shibo who rowed me off the wharf. She was spit-hard. But these two aren't much better.

We're turning left at the old power station.

Gobbo gives a cough, takes one hand off the steering wheel, pulls out a cig, lights it. Winds down the window, leaves it open. Cold air jets into the van. I pull my coat around me. Think of the knives inside. And then it hits me.

How come I only just thought of 'em?

The knives, I mean. How come I didn't think of 'em earlier? When there was danger. The shibo in the boat, these nebs in the van. How come my hands aren't already fixed on the blades like they used to be?

Yeah. Used to be.

Am I changing, Bigeyes?

Cos once upon a time I didn't need to think about the knives. I told you that before. My hands just went there by themselves. Only now, here I am in danger, and my hands . . .

They're just resting by my side.

And I haven't even thought about the knives.

Till this moment.

Maybe I'm cutting loose from 'em.

Or they're cutting loose from me.

Don't much care which. Long as it happens. Cos one thing I know, Bigeyes. Whatever I can do with a knife, it's not worth dog shit now. Won't save me. Not really. Not the part of me that matters anyway. The part old Mary found. And little Jaz.

And Becky. Sweet, beautiful Becky.

None of them ever needed a knife. So why do I?

I reach inside my coat, pull 'em out, hold 'em up. Look over at the shibos. They haven't even noticed. They've forgotten about me. Still naffing like before, into each other's ears, softer than the engine.

Gobbo hasn't noticed either. Takes a last drag of his cig, flicks the butt out of the window, lights another. Drives on, watching the dawn.

I stare at the knives again.

I've thrown 'em away before, Bigeyes. And every time they've come back. But maybe this time'll be different. Maybe this time I'll really cut loose. And be free.

I throw 'em towards the front of the van. They clunk on the floor, slide along it, disappear under the driver's seat. The janxes stop talking, fix me for a moment. Gobbo does the same in his mirror. Then back again, like before.

Janxes go on talking.

Gobbo goes on smoking. And watching the dawn.

They don't even know what I threw. And they don't care either.

I ease myself down, curl up on the floor of the van. Doesn't matter where these nebs are taking me. I don't give two bells any more. Something hard's pressing into my side. Feel round with my hand. It's the gun, digging into me. Scrab it tight, chuck it after the knives.

Close my eyes.

Sleep.

Wake. Or rather get woken. Gobbo's voice, blasting over me.

'Get up!'

The black gobbo, leaning close. Breath stinks of cigs.

'Get up!' he bawls.

'Piss off!'

A hand clips me on the cheek, does it again. I blink my eyes open, spit up at him. I was dreaming of Becky. Sweet, darling Becky. And now this jerk's gone and—

Whap!

He clips me again, harder. Then growls into my ear.

'You don't spit at me. And you don't tell me to piss off. You don't never do that.'

Grabs me by the collar, yanks me up till I'm sitting. I stare at him, still clutching the picture of Becky in my head, and her smile, her beautiful smile. Only now it's fading and I got this bum glaring at me instead. Van's stopped, back door's open. He's standing outside it, leaning in, the two shibos just behind him.

And Ruby.

Behind them.

'Don't hurt him,' she says.

'Why not?' mutters the black guy. 'He got no

manners. He got your girl killed. He don't care about nobody. Not you, not Becky—'

I feel my fist snap out. Can't stop it. Moment he said Becky's name.

I hit him hard in the face. Doesn't hurt him but it takes him by surprise. He gives a roar, pulls back his arm, fist clenched. Ruby yells.

'Seth!'

It's not a request. It's a command. No question. And the gobbo obeys it.

Just.

He's got his fist back ready, and it's shaking, shaking. His body's shaking too. He's got his eyes fixed on me, his mouth spitting hate. He wants to kill me. He wants to slam me into the darkness so I never come back.

'Seth.'

Ruby again, quieter this time. She comes forward, pushes between the two shibos, slips a hand round the big guy's fist, eases it back down. Then leans in to the van, fixes me. And slaps me hard in the face.

'Get out of the van,' she mutters. 'And keep your mouth shut.'

I get out of the van. Have to push round the black gobbo, cos he's not moving. But he doesn't hurt me. Just glowers into my face. I step back from him, and the others, check round. We're in a garage, multi-storey, basement level, I'm guessing.

Nobody else here. Plenty of space, just a couple of other motors, empty, and this van. Look back at Ruby and the others. Just the four of 'em. Seth, Ruby, and the two shibos.

Watching me.

Sound of an engine. I check round again. Car pulling in, wheels screaming. Two black guys in the front, shibo in the back. The one who rowed me off the wharf.

Just what I don't need.

They squeal up, stop, get out.

Join the others.

All watching me.

'Let's go,' says Ruby.

The others turn towards the exit. Ruby stays put, her eyes on me.

'That means you,' she mutters.

I walk up to her.

'And keep your mouth shut,' she says.

I follow her, through the exit, up the steps. I was right. Basement level. We cut up the stairway, nobody talking. Silence feels strange, kind of threatening. Don't know why, Bigeyes, but it's like they're all waiting for me to speak.

Keep your mouth shut, Ruby said. But I don't think she means that. Keep it shut now, yeah, but not later. There's talking to come, and it's coming from me, and they all want to hear it. Don't ask me how I know. And till they get to listen, nobody's going to speak.

So the silence goes on.

As we walk.

Out of the multi-storey, round the back of the shops, through the estate, out the other side. I know this place, Bigeyes. Not well, I mean not really well, like I know the rest of the Beast. We're way south here, right on the outskirts of the bastard. But I've been here a few times.

Scragland.

That's what I call this area. Dronky shops, dronky estates. Nobody's got any jippy round here. We're cutting left, round the little park, out the other side. Day's waking up. Don't know what time it is.

Haven't seen a clock and I'm not going to ask any of this lot. No sun in sight. Just a grey, chilly sky. Far off in the north I can feel the Beast snorting. Even out here I got his smell choking me, like Seth's ciggy breath.

Turning left, down a little street. Terrace houses, crumbly and old. Sound of televisions on, radios, man shouting at a kid in one of the kitchens. We trig on past, now right, through a gate, through a walled garden, binbags and rubbish all around, and up to the back door of a house.

It opens as we reach it.

And there's another gobbo standing there.

Old guy, black like the others. Don't know him but he looks familiar. Then I guess it.

'Hello, Poppa,' says Ruby.

He doesn't answer. Just stands there, looking out. Nothing wrong with his head. I'm telling you, Bigeyes. He's got all his fizz. I know why he's not moving. He's looking out, looking for one thing.

Me.

We fix eyes.

And I look down. It's no good, Bigeyes. I just can't do it. I can't look Becky's grandpa in the face. Specially now, when I'm not prepared. I didn't know she had a grandpa. She never told me. But then, you know what?

That's kind of how it was.

I'm only just getting that now.

We never really talked about her. Yeah, yeah, we talked about what she was doing at school. But that's only cos she was trying to help me. She loved school and she wanted me to go with her. So we talked about that.

Or she did.

But we never talked about her. Not properly. We only ever talked about me. Me, me, bloody me. And she was cute about that. You know why? Cos all she ever wanted to do was help me. Get me out of trouble, make me better, make me worth something.

Stead of what I am now.

Worth nothing.

I look up. I make myself. And there's the old gobbo still watching me. His eyes don't move. And I know he knows. About how Becky died. Ruby's rung him, texted him, whatever. He knows. He must hate me so bad.

'You better come in,' he murmurs.

Deep voice, quiet, sort of thoughtful.

They walk in, slow, nobody talking. And it's just like before, Bigeyes. Like they're waiting. For me. Yeah, that's right. It's me got to break the silence. Only not yet. Not till they're ready for it.

And they'll show me when they are.

They file through, into the house.

I follow. I don't want to. And I could get away easy. I'm last in and nobody's looking back at me. But I walk on. I know I got to. Into the lounge and there they are all standing there.

Old Poppa, Ruby holding his hand. The big guy, Seth, still raging at me. The two janxes from the back of the van, the hard shibo with the piercings who rowed me off the wharf. Miss Spikyface. And the two new dronks.

Yeah, and now I recognize 'em.

The motor cruiser. One at the wheel, the other coiling rope. And now that bit's starting to make sense. The old boat chuffing off into Mother Grime. It was a

45

decoy. They sent me in the dinghy with Spikyface and she got me up the steps to the van. But they used the motor cruiser to distract any grinks who might be looking.

Ruby made her way here on her own.

Or something like that.

Whatever.

I'm here. And these nebs are here. And Jesus, Bigeyes. Someone else is here. Someone I just noticed behind me. On the mantelpiece.

Becky.

Oh, Christ.

Same photo as Ruby's got in her little shrine at home.

Same smiling face.

I look away. Can't bear to see it. And feel the guilt.

Poppa sits down on the sofa, Ruby next to him, hand on his knee. The others sit down too—Spikyface in the armchair, dronks on the floor, janxes flopped against 'em, one either side.

Nobody moves. Nobody lights a cig, makes tea. They just watch me. And wait. I'm still standing. I glance at Becky, feel the guilt again. Sit down on the floor, in front of the old man.

He looks back at me and there's something in his eyes. Something . . . I don't know . . . something I haven't seen much in my life. A piece of Ruby, yeah, and Becky, but it's not just that. It's something else. I've seen it in Jaz too. And Mary.

It's something they all got.

And I haven't.

Am I imagining this, Bigeyes? No, I'm not. It's there. It's definitely there. That . . . thing they all got. That special . . . thing. And I know I got to hold onto it. Cos I might never see it again.

I don't want to call it love, cos it's not love. But I'll tell you one thing.

It's the opposite of hate.

The old man reaches out, takes Ruby's hand.

Fixes me with his eyes.

'It's time to talk,' he says. 'About Becky. And those men who are trying to kill you.'

So I talk. And I do something I never meant to do.

Certainly not to these nebs. I tell the whole story. Yeah, Bigeyes. The whole effing lot. More than I ever told Bex or Bannerman or anybody.

It just comes flooding out. Like I can't stop it.

And suddenly I don't want to.

I tell 'em about the home I first lived in, how I got found outside. And what happened to me inside, even though I can only imagine it. I tell 'em about burning the place down, running away, getting into trouble.

Hawk getting hold of me. What he trained me to do. Killing, I mean. And how good I was. That's right, Bigeyes. I give 'em numbers. I count 'em out, all the dead dronks. And I give 'em Hawk's name. Yeah, you bet. I want 'em to know.

Lord Haffler-Devereaux.

I say it twice. I spell it. I say it again. I tell 'em what he looks like, how he talks, how he thinks. What he likes to do with small boys. What he did with me.

I tell 'em about Becky. How I loved her, how I still love her, how I'll always love her. I tell 'em about seeing her die, running away, playing dead in the old city. I tell 'em about Trixi and the troll-gang. And Mary. The bungalow, the grinks catching up with me. I tell 'em about Bex, and little Jaz.

Riff finding me, Dig getting killed.

And Jaz taken.

Coming back here, to the effing stinking Beast. Kidnapping Hawk's boy, getting Jaz back. And then seeing her taken away for ever. Like it's meant to be. Like it's always meant to be. Cos that's how it is, Bigeyes. Everyone I care about gets taken away. Becky, Jaz, Mary. Everyone.

I go on talking. No one stops me. They just listen. I talk about the Game, the power play that's smashing up this world. I talk about the slimeheads at the top and the low-life underneath. I talk about Ezi and Spit, how I cranked up Nelson and the other gangster bojos.

How I got in touch with Bannerman. I tell 'em what I told him, what I wrote down for Ezi and Spit, what the gangster bosses round the Beast now know. I tell 'em about Pink getting shot. And how there's going to be more. Loads more.

Then suddenly I stop. I look up at the photo of Becky.

And burst into tears.

I didn't mean to. But it's like the talking. It just came flooding out and now I can't stop it. I close my eyes, dip my head, hug my knees into my chest. I feel my body shake as I howl into the dark.

Don't know how long it lasts.

Just feels like it's for ever.

When I open my eyes again, they've all gone. I'm still hugging my knees but I've stopped crying, stopped shaking. My eyes are blurry with tears. I wipe 'em with my sleeve, sniff hard. Feel a hand touch the top of my head.

Then go.

It's Ruby. Can't see her but I know it's her. Standing behind me. I look round, peer up at her. She's frowning, lips tight together. I wipe my eyes again.

'I'm sorry,' I murmur.

The tears bubble back.

'I'm sorry.'

I squeeze my eyes tight as they'll go. The hand touches my head again, hesitates. I feel it wanting to go. I reach up, grab it, hold it there.

Go on crying.

The hand stays. It doesn't stroke.

But it stays.

I hear 'em come back in the room. Some of 'em anyway. I don't bother looking. Too busy crying. But I'm easing off now. Not sobbing any more, just whimpering like Hawk's kid when he was curled up in the car and thought I was going to kill him. Don't ask me why I'm thinking of Damien at a time like this.

Ruby's hand goes. I open my eyes again, look up. She's walking back to the sofa. The two janxes have come back and the dronks who rolled up in the car. Nobody else.

Sound of a radio playing down the corridor. Clattery kitchen noises, Poppa's voice, low and slow. A sharp, snappy laugh. Got to be Spikyface. Throaty chuckle from Seth. Poppa's voice again. Can't clap what he's saying.

I look over at Ruby. She's sat down on the sofa. Other four are sprawled on the floor again. Steps in the corridor. Seth and Spiky come in. Ruby glances up at 'em.

'He sent us back,' says Spiky.

'Said he don't want no help,' mutters Seth.

Ruby doesn't answer. Just watches 'em sit down on the floor.

Then turns to me.

'So what was his name?' she says. 'Or don't you know it?'

She's narrowed her eyes and she's checking me close. I know what she wants, Bigeyes. The guy who shot Becky. And yeah, I do know his name. You bet I do.

The clattering goes on in the kitchen. Radio still playing but Poppa's changing channels. I hardly listen. All I hear is the silence in this room, and my own fear shrieking inside it.

Becky looks down from the mantelpiece. I look back and there's that thing in her face. The opposite of hate. The thing that can't be love. I look back at Ruby.

'Ricky Dean,' I tell her. 'That's the guy's name. But they all called him Milky. Cos of his hair.'

She stiffens, looks round at the others.

'You heard of this guy?'

They shake their heads. She looks quickly back at me.

'You got an address?'

'It's no good you going—'

'I'm not going no place.' She glares at me. 'I'm sending the police round.'

'Ruby—'

'Just cos it happened three years ago don't mean—'

'Ruby—'

'Don't mean it's too late for justice—'

'Ruby, he's dead.'

Silence again. I feel 'em all staring at me. Clattering sounds come back. Some part of me picks up that the radio's gone off. And there's footsteps in the corridor again. Moving slow.

'He's dead, Ruby,' I say. 'Cos I killed him.'

She breathes in sharp. Poppa appears in the doorway, holding a tray. Walks over to me, bends with an effort, rests it on the floor. I look down at it. Tatty old thing, stained and peeling. Chipped blue plate on it with sausages, beans, eggs, mush. Knife and fork. Glass of orange juice. Napkin in a little red holder.

Got Becky's name on it.

Oh, Jesus.

Poppa nods me towards the food.

'Eat,' he murmurs.

I pick up the knife and fork. Don't touch the napkin. Can't do it. Feel like it's wrong. Whatever the old man means by it. I start eating. Poppa doesn't move away. Clears his throat. Deep, slow sound, like the way he talks. I look up at him, snap the meaning from his eyes.

But it's no good. I still can't do it.

He starts to bend down. Big effort like before. I can't let him do this.

'OK,' I say quickly.

He stops, halfway down, his eyes still on me. And there's something in 'em makes the guilt even worse.

'OK,' I say again.

And I pick up the napkin holder. He straightens up, rubbing his lower back. Stands over me, looking down. Big, sad eyes, same as Ruby's. I pull the napkin out of the holder, feel the tears splutter inside me again.

'Eat,' says the old man.

He's still watching me. I'm still watching him. I take a breath and somehow the tears stay back. Poppa moves off, sits down on the sofa next to Ruby. She rests her head on his shoulder. I spread the napkin on my lap, smooth it out, gentle as I can. Put the holder back on the tray. Look up at Becky's photo.

Start eating again.

Room stays quiet. No one talks till I've finished and pushed the tray aside. Then Poppa leans forward.

'There been more violence in the city,' he says.

The old man doesn't hurry. Takes his time with the words. Tells us what he heard on the radio before we got here, what he heard while he was cooking.

First up, the porkers have found the diamonds and art stuff I left in my hiding places back in the old city. Bannerman must have got 'em onto that bung-quick cos Poppa heard it on the news at six this morning. Massive haul of stolen artefacts, worth a fortune. Jesus, Bigeyes, they got it.

But the Beast's the place where it's really ripping up.

Three more shootings. No names mentioned but it sounds like high-level dronks. I'm guessing the top three spikes on Ezi's list. Nelson won't have cracked them on his own. He'll have needed help from the other gangster bosses, so that means Fitz and Spice at least are in it, and maybe some of the other bojos, and all their dregs.

Hawk'll know he's in a fight now.

But it won't be enough on its own. The bastard's too smart. The moment this stuff hit the news Hawk'll have pulled up the drawbridge and hidden anything that could shunt him.

No, Bigeyes.

It's down to the backup hard drive from Hawk's computer.

If Bannerman's lifted that too, we got a chance.

Poppa goes on talking, in his soft, slow voice, rolling out the words he's snagged from the radio bulletins. Police investigation, criminal network. Still no names mentioned. Then I catch one.

Mine.

And see Poppa looking straight at me again.

'Every news bulletin,' he says, 'your name get spoken. They all talking about the boy called Blade.'

The others look round at him, then at me.

Poppa narrows his eyes.

'It's time to choose,' he says.

I know it is, Bigeyes. And I know exactly what he means. Cut loose from knives, from killing, from everything I've been. Or stay the same. And go on suffering even more. But Poppa doesn't put it that way.

'You can come with me,' he says, 'and we go find this Mr Bannerman. Or you can just go now. Walk out the door. Wherever you want to go.'

The old man pauses, goes on.

'And I go talk to Mr Bannerman by myself.'

Silence. I feel the others watching me hard. But I keep my eyes on Poppa. I know what he wants, Bigeyes. He wants me to go with him. He doesn't want me to choose the head start.

Somebody's mobile chinks. I see Ruby reach into her pocket, check a text. Poppa goes on watching me. And you know what, Bigeyes? Suddenly it's like Mary's watching me too, sitting there with the old man, urging me to do what he wants.

I glance up at Becky.

Yeah, sweetheart. It's what you want too, isn't it?

It's what everyone wants.

I look back at Poppa. His face is so grave. He shakes his head.

'No point running no more,' he murmurs. 'You done some bad and you got to face up to that. But you done some good too. You must not forget that. So let's you and me go find Mr Bannerman.'

Before I can answer, Ruby cuts in.

And the panic in her voice makes us all sit up.

'Bex is in trouble.'

I stare at her.

'What's happened?'

'I give her my mobile number. When you first left her with me. Made her write it down. Case she ever needed it.'

'But what's happened?'

'She just sent me a text. It's written bad but I worked it out.'

'What does she say?'

'She been beat up and she's run away again. Got some guys looking for her. She's scared out of her head.'

'Where is she?'

'Hiding in my back garden. Says she can't get in the house cos she can't find the spare key.'

Ruby frowns.

'But I told her where it is. I showed her. Before she ran off.'

She's freaked out, Bigeyes. She's forgotten where the key is cos she's too choked to think. We got to help her, got to do something. Ruby's already on her feet.

'Poppa, you take care of Blade. Rest of us got to go look for Bex.'

'I'm coming with you,' I say.

'No, you ain't,' says Ruby. 'Poppa just give you two choices. And coming with us ain't one of 'em.'

'I'm still coming.'

Ruby takes no notice, turns to the others.

'Seth, get the van. Wait for us by the shops.'

'What about our motor?' says Spiky.

'Best we all go in the van,' says Ruby. 'Poppa's going to need the motor to drive Blade to the police station.'

'I'm not going to the police station,' I say. 'I'm coming with you.'

I feel 'em all turn, fix me. But most of all I feel

Poppa's eyes. They're the only ones not angry with me. But I'm forgetting Becky. Her eyes aren't angry either. They never were.

'I got to come with you,' I say. 'For Bex's sake. Cos I can help her. I can tell her about Jaz being all right. Bex'll want to know. That little girl means everything to her. Everything in the world. And she'll want to hear it from me. Cos I saw Jaz face to face. You got to let me come. For Bex's sake.'

Ruby frowns, then bungs a glance at the others.

'Go get the van and the motor.'

They crash out of the room and suddenly there's just me, Poppa and Ruby left. And Becky, watching quiet. Ruby turns away, punches a number into her mobile, put it to her ear, waits.

Poppa's eyes settle on me again.

But he says nothing.

Ruby gabs into the phone.

'Bex, it's me, Ruby. Listen, if you get this message, we're coming, OK? You're going to be fine. We're on our way. And Blade's with us and he's coming too. He's going to tell you all about Jaz. Cos she's cool, yeah? She's safe. She's with good people and she's safe. So we're coming and we're going to look after you. Now listen good. The key—it's under the brick just behind the bin. You got that? Under the brick. Just behind the bin. Now you go get that key and you let yourself in, then you lock the door again and go upstairs to the bedroom, and you wait for us there. Don't turn the lights on and keep away from the windows. You got that? We're coming now and I'm keeping my mobile on, case you want to ring. Be strong, girl. You're going to be fine.'

She hangs up, turns back to us, frowns again.

'Am I doing this wrong, Poppa? With Blade, I mean.'

She peers into his face like a small girl.

Like Becky almost.

Yeah, like Becky.

The old man takes a long, slow breath. Like he's counting out the ones he's still got left. Then looks straight at me.

'Only Blade knows if this is right or wrong,' he says.

There's another silence. Too deep to feel comfortable.

'I'll come straight back,' I say. 'I promise I will. I'll come straight back. And go with you to Inspector Bannerman.'

I look him hard in the face. I want him to believe me. I want that so much.

Poppa looks back.

And says nothing.

Van rumbles through the grey morning. I'm slumped in the back next to Ruby with Spiky sitting opposite. Seth's driving like before. Nobody with him in the front. The janxes have gone in the motor with the two dronks.

Can't say I miss 'em.

Only problem is I got Spiky fixing me with those eyes.

Ruby's trying Bex's mobile again. But she's still getting voicemail. Leaves another message, hangs up. I'm trembling. Can't think straight. All I got in my head is Bex.

I can't crack this, Bigeyes. This . . . caring. Cos it's back again, right? Caring about Becky, Jaz, Mary, that's cute. I get that. But caring about Bex? Of all people. I didn't think she meant anything to me. But she does.

I can't bear to think of her shivering in Ruby's garden.

I just want to get to her quick. I want to tell her about Jaz. Cos you know what? That'll pick her straight up. She'll fight back then. She was never busting with grit. You seen that for yourself. She's not yellow, like Trixi used to say. I found that out bung-quick. There's no way that girl's yellow.

But she's not busting with grit.

So I'm going to tell her about Jaz. And you just watch her get better. She'll be fizzing when she's heard about Jaz. And I'll tell you something else, Bigeyes. I'm going to get Bex sorted, make sure Ruby's got her safe, then I'm heading back to Poppa. And I'm going to prove to him I meant what I said.

We're going straight to Bannerman.

And I'm going to give myself up.

'You was brave,' says a voice.

I look up, startled. Spiky's watching me from the other side of the van. Her eyes seem to prick the inside of my head.

'What you told us about kidnapping that boy,' she says. 'And getting Jaz back. You was brave.'

I stare at her, not sure what to say.

If anything.

She watches me a moment longer, then turns her head.

We drive on, heading towards Ruby's district. That's right, Bigeyes. The Den, remember? One big shithole. Least we got muscle with us this time. But I'm still worried sick about Bex. She found her way to Ruby's house. That part of her's still working.

But what's happened to her? Beaten up, she said. Question is—how bad and who by? And who's after her now?

Spiky calls out suddenly.

'Seth!'

'What's up, babe?'

'Who left them knives there?'

'What knives?'

'Under your seat. I can see 'em from here.'

'They're mine,' I cut in.

Spiky fixes me again. I catch Seth's eye in the mirror too. I look down.

'They're mine,' I say. 'Only they're not.'

'What you talking about?' says Spiky.

'I threw 'em away.'

'You what?'

'I don't want 'em. You can have 'em if you want. There's a gun under there too. Seth's gun. Take the lot.'

I look up, drill her eyes. 'Got a problem with that?'

'No,' she says.

'Good.'

I look away. Can't face her. Can't face any of 'em.

And I can't face the knives. Not any more. Not ever again.

I feel Ruby take my hand. I flip my head, fix her. And there's that thing in her face again. The thing I want so much. The opposite of hate. I feel a shudder, stare into her eyes, try to think of another way of saying sorry.

A better way. But it's no good. I just can't.

She lets go of my hand, touches my cheek.

Turns away too.

Van thunders on, closer to the Den, into the Den. Ruby's calling directions now, taking us there by a dronky route. But I know what she's doing. She's making sure we don't get clapped too easy. Cos there's guys out there, Bex said.

Hunting her.

And we don't want 'em hunting us too.

Seth's slowing down and we're all watching out. Ruby's up in the front now, next to the big guy.

'Left,' she mutters.

Seth turns left, chunks through the gears.

'Not too fast,' says Ruby.

He stays in third, lets us rumble down. I know where we are. You bet. And Ruby's playing it just right. We'll come at her house from the back. I'm guessing she'll take us down Regency Road, stack the van and trig us through the estate.

'Left again,' she says.

Told you, Bigeyes. Down Regency Road, on to the end. Seth's braking.

'Pull over,' says Ruby. 'By the wall.'

He pulls over, turns off the engine. We don't get out. Ruby's on her mobile again. Tries Bex's number first. Voicemail again. Tries another number. I'm guessing the dronks who went in the motor with the two janxes.

'You got there?' she goes.

Silence while she listens.

'OK,' she says. 'Meet us where I said.'

Hangs up, looks round at us.

'Let's go.'

Out of the van and here's the back of the shopping precinct. Not too many nebs out yet. Couple of old dunnies pushing trolleys. Girl in school uniform. Stuffs a shiver round my heart cos it makes me think of Becky.

Same uniform, same school.

But I can't think about that now and Ruby's striding on anyway. I can feel her fretting, like I'm doing. Bex is close but Christ knows what state she'll be in. She might even be dead.

She hasn't answered her phone.

And you'd think she'd be checking. She should have got Ruby's messages by now. I can feel my heart pounding as I speed up. But I'm still glancing round. It's not just Bex who's in danger here. I got to think of myself too. Even with these three for support.

No sign of the nebs from the motor. I didn't see Ruby fix anything with 'em. Maybe she texted while I wasn't looking. She did something anyway. Cos suddenly here they are, waiting on the other side of the precinct.

The two dronks anyway.

The janxes have disappeared.

'You done what I told you?' says Ruby.

Guy with the dreads answers.

'We left the girls outside the house.'

'Where exactly?'

'Over the street, down the little lane. Like you said. They can see the house but they're out of sight. They'll text if any shit turns up.'

'Any sign of Bex?'

Guy shakes his head. Seth flexes his muscles.

'Let's go,' he grunts.

'Wait,' says Ruby.

She holds out a hand, stops him. And now she's looking round. Yeah, Bigeyes, and I know why. She's got that same feeling I got. A feeling I've had many times.

When you know something's wrong but you can't see it.

We're all checking round now. No sign of trouble.

Nebs coming and going but they're all muffins so far. Can't work out what's wrong. But that's often how it is, Bigeyes. You can't work it out. You just know.

Ruby catches my eye.

And something passes between us. Something I haven't seen before. Not from her anyway. She's checking what I got. What I'm picking up. Cos she knows I crack stuff most nebs don't. She's watching me close, looking for anything I can give her.

Or maybe just reassurance. That she's playing this cute. I guess it's respect. But that's not what matters right now. Bex is what matters. Ruby's still watching me.

'What you getting?' she says.

'Nothing. But I don't feel right.'

She doesn't answer, just goes on checking round. Couple of kids run past, gobbo walking a dog. Three dunnies, naffing. One looks us over as they plod by. Ruby watches 'em go, turns to us.

'Let's go,' she mutters.

We trig on, over the car park, down the alleyway, round the corner to where the back gardens start. Ruby stops, checks again. We're all flicking round, watching for scum.

But nobody's here.

Alleyway's deserted.

Apart from a cat. Then that wigs it too.

I run my eye down as far as the street. No sign of movement there, no cars even. We walk on, slow, checking as we go. Even Spiky looks nervous. I glance at Seth, just in front of me. He looks bigger, meaner, and so do the two dronks in front of him. I got to admit I'm glad they're here.

But I still don't feel right.

Gate on our left. First of the back gardens. We walk past it, past the next, and the next. And here's Ruby's. I stare at it. Feels weird, Bigeyes. You know why? I'll give you another confession. Yeah, yeah. Another one.

I waited out here once.

For Becky.

That's right. Just once. When she wasn't supposed to be seeing me. She sneaked out in secret just to talk to me. We didn't go off anywhere. She had homework to do and didn't have time. And she felt guilty not telling Ruby.

So I waited for her here.

And she slipped out and we slumped down against the wall.

And talked soft, so no one could hear us.

Then she went back in.

I remember sitting here after she'd gone. Just sitting and dreaming about her. She never knew. Cos I never told her. She'll have thought I just ran straight off. Back to my dirty life of crime. All the bad stuff she wanted me to stop.

But I didn't run straight off.

I stayed here, slumped against the wall.

For hours. Just dreaming of Becky.

I look at Ruby. And feel the guilt again.

She looks back. And for a moment I think she's clapped what I'm feeling. But it's not that. It's the other thing. Wanting what I got. What I'm picking up. I look back at her, listen, wait.

Feel.

'Still not right, Ruby.'

She's thinking the same, Bigeyes. Check her face. She knows something's wrong. But I'll tell you something. She's going to take us in.

Don't ask me how I know.

'Let's go,' she murmurs.

See?

In through the gate.

Bex isn't in the garden.

Stop, check round.

Poky little space, no grass, just concrete slabs piled high with cardboard boxes Ruby's never got round to shunting. Becky's bike propped up in the corner, covered with a piece of canvas and tied under the frame to keep it there.

Even from here I can see it's rusting underneath.

Check out the house. No sounds from inside. Nearest window's the kitchen. I bung a glance at it. No sign of anybody inside. Eyeshine up the wall to the top window. Glint into the landing but nothing more.

Not Bex anyway.

Ruby pulls up the brick behind the bin, checks underneath.

'Key's gone,' she says.

Straightens up, fixes me. I know the look now.

'She's not in there, Ruby.'

'How do you know?'

'I just do.'

'So who's in the house if she's not?'

'Don't know.'

She goes on watching me. I feel Spiky shift close by, and the two dronks. Seth flexes his muscles again. Ruby snaps a glance at him.

'Stay here with Blade,' she tells him. 'Keep your eyes open. If there's trouble, get him away.' Fixes the others. 'You three come with me.'

And before I can say anything, she unlocks the back door and cuts into the house. Spiky's straight after her, followed by the two dronks. I start forward. Can't help it, Bigeyes. I know Bex isn't in there. Might be nobody in there.

But there might be scum waiting.

And it's not right Ruby and the others should take it alone.

But now everything changes. Seth picks it up at the same time. Not from the road but the way we just came, down the alleyway.

Footsteps.

Running towards us.

'Come on,' says Seth.

'We got to warn the others.'

'No time. Got to get you away.'

He pulls me back towards the gate. I chuck a look at the house. Back door's closed and no sign of Ruby and the others crashing back out. They won't have heard what we've heard. But maybe that's as well. They got to stay trimmed on what's in there.

'Come on, boy!' says Seth.

He's yanking me out of the gate now, into the alleyway. Sound of feet's getting louder but no sign yet of who's coming. Only one way to go and that's to the street. We hare down the alleyway, Ruby's house on our left, and still I'm glancing at it, even as I run. I'm desperate for a glimpse of what's going on inside.

But there's no one to be seen.

From behind us comes a shout.

'There!'

I don't look back and neither does Seth. We pile down the alleyway, burst into the street and—shit! Car ploughing in from the left, van from the right. But they're not grinks.

They're porkers.

No sirens, just a scream of brakes, then doors opening, feet slamming the pavement. Seth's got a hand round my arm and he's rushing me away down the road. But it's no good.

I'm slow and he's worse.

Footsteps grow louder. They're closing in fast. Seth goes down. Someone's tackled him from behind. I feel arms lock round me, hoist me off the ground. I kick out but it makes no difference. Guy's too strong and there's another porker ripping in to help him.

Seth's on his feet again, fighting like a bear, but there's three gobbos pinning him back against the wall, heavy bastards, and they know what they're doing.

'Ease off, big man,' says one. 'It's not you we want.'

He takes no notice, struggles to break free. They snag his arms up his back, kick his legs away, drop him to his knees. I call out as the other two bundle me off.

'Leave it, Seth. Nothing you can do.'

He still goes on fighting.

'Seth, leave it, mate.'

I don't see what happens to him. Or what's happening with Ruby in the house. It's fizzing too quick, Bigeyes. I'm over the gobbo's shoulder, bouncing as he carries me to the van. I feel the air spinning, the world spinning with it.

And somewhere in the middle, a picture of Becky.

Perfectly still.

But then it's gone. I'm tumbling into the back of the van, the porker climbing in after me. There's a click of cuffs, a roar of the engine, and we're tearing off down the street.

Right at the junction, down to the crossing, left past the school. I keep my head down, tracking the streets in my mind. One thing's bung-clear. We're not heading for the nearest police station.

I check the porkers.

Only two, both gobbos. Guy next to me's staring down at the floor of the van. Other gobbo's at the wheel, eyes on the road. I look up at the mirror. No sign of him watching me.

Neither talking.

Flick a glance at the cuffs. Gobbo got 'em on me pretty cute. I'll give him that. My right hand, his left. Frisked me good too. Quick and smart. I think of Poppa. It's what he wanted, I guess. Me going with the porkers. And I was going to give myself up anyway, straight after sorting Bex.

So why doesn't this feel right?

Why don't these gobbos feel right?

I'm thinking, Bigeyes, specially now we're heading away from the next nearest police station. I'm thinking about that business with Bex. Like they knew I was coming. Or loaded the stakes so high in their favour it was worth a punt sending the motors.

Case I turned up.

Like I did.

Something's wrong, Bigeyes.

They're porkers, these guys. No messing. I always know. I've seen too many. And this is a porker van. But what kind of porkers are they? Something feels wrong, Bigeyes. I'm telling you.

We've changed direction again. Not even heading towards the centre of the Beast. Driver's taking us down the east side. We're still north of Mother Grime and cracking in fast, but I got a feeling we're not crossing over.

Told you.

Cutting left, down the underpass, up the other side, left again.

There's no police station down this way, Bigeyes. Not unless the driver's lost. Which he's not. And another thing. No messages getting sent to HQ. Not from these gobbos. Not official messages anyway. They're sitting quiet, like they've been told to say nothing, just do the business.

Yeah, the business.

But what kind of business?

I'm starting to guess the answer.

Right at the lights, over the roundabout, left down the lane towards the warehouses. I've been round here before, Bigeyes, and I got a bad feeling. Picture of Becky floats into my head again.

And floats out just as quick.

Cos we've stopped.

Driver trigs round the back, opens the door. I clamber out, best I can with the cuff plucking at the other guy's hand. He climbs out with me and now we're walking, over a courtyard, high walls all around, warehouses beyond 'em.

'Funny-looking police station,' I chirp.

They don't answer. We're heading for a gate in the wall, through it, left down a little path, round the back of a building. It's not a warehouse. It's an old office block. In through a side door, down a corridor. Nobody else here.

But the place isn't empty.

I'm telling you, Bigeyes. It's not empty.

Through a door, down another corridor. More narrow than the last. Gobbo with the cuff goes ahead, pulling me after him. Driver tramps behind. I think of the other porkers, the ones wrestling with Seth.

Didn't hear 'em motor after us.

And I'm getting the reason why.

They were just there for the muscle. To make sure of the catch. These two are the delivery boys. And now it's time. To see who wants me.

Door opens and there's the room.

A small, windowless office. Grey, sparse. Filing cabinet in the corner, coat stand next to it. Second door over to the right and just up from that a desk with a gobbo behind it. A senior police officer from his uniform.

Very senior.

But I already know who this is. The face tells me everything. You couldn't miss the resemblance if you tried. But I'd worked out who it was before I got here.

Bex's father.

'Jakes,' I murmur.

He stiffens slightly, bridles even, then gives a smile, leans back in his chair, purrs at me.

'I generally insist on people using my full title. Out of respect for the high office I have the honour to hold.'

He flicks an eye up at the two porkers, then back at me.

'And if that respect is not forthcoming, then I instruct others to do whatever is necessary to produce it.'

I don't answer. I'm still skimming his face. So like Bex's in one way. But nothing like it in others. I think of what she told me. About what he did to her. What he's maybe still doing to her.

But even without knowing that I'd take this guy for slime.

He's still watching me close. I got a feeling he's waiting. For that respect he's just threatened to beat out of me. He glances up at the porkers, pauses. I brace myself. Jakes catches my eye and I feel him smile again.

But it's a hidden smile this time. Just under the eyes.

He looks at the porkers again.

Nods.

I brace myself a second time.

But nothing smashes into my face. Instead the porker with the cuffs tugs me over to the wall by the desk, jerks my arm down, uncuffs his own hand, clips the bracelet onto the radiator, stands back.

And hands Jakes the key.

Jakes pulls open a drawer, drops the key inside, leaves the drawer open.

Gives a flick of his head.

The two porkers trig out of the room, the way we came in. I hear their steps crunching down the corridor, fading, fading. A few moments later, the sound of the van revving up, driving off.

Silence.

Just me standing here, chained to the radiator, and Jakes sitting behind the desk. Watching. Then he reaches into the drawer again. Pulls out a hammer.

I stiffen. Can't help it. Been trying not to flinch but I can't stop it. He catches my fear, smirks, stands up, hammer in his right hand. Walks round to me, stops close by, sits on the edge of the desk.

Easy reach.

Nothing I can do, Bigeyes. They set this up too well. I got my right hand locked and no room to use my left. And that's weak anyway. I take a breath, deep, hard. I got to face up to this dreg.

Whatever he does to me.

He's seen my fear once.

He mustn't see it again.

I twist round, face him best I can. Get ready to spit, snarl, whatever.

He speaks.

'I've been curious to meet you for some time. After all I've heard. And the things Rebecca told me.'

'She told me a few things about you too.'

'She's a little unstable, you know.'

'What have you done to her?'

He looks amused by this.

'How can I do anything to her,' he says, 'when I don't know where she is?'

Shit, Bigeyes. So she really did run away. If this bastard's telling the truth. And then suddenly I clap it. What I kind of suspected all along.

'You sent that text,' I murmur. 'To Ruby. Made out it was from Bex.'

He looks amused again. And I know straightaway I'm right.

'You got everything you needed to know from Bex,' I say. 'Don't tell me how. She ran away again. And you thought if you texted Ruby, I might just show up with her at the house. If you made Bex sound desperate enough.'

He looks down at the hammer, plays with it.

Chuckles.

I try to think. Got to be something I can throw at this slug.

'I've been in touch with Inspector Bannerman,' I start.

'Ah, yes,' he goes. 'Inspector Bannerman. As he was once known.'

'What's that supposed to mean?'

Jakes taps the hammer on the side of the desk, chuckles again.

'I'm afraid you won't find him an *Inspector* Bannerman any more. Such a sad end to a promising career but you know, alcohol dependence does terrible things. Distorts a man's judgement. It was only a matter of time before he did something disastrous. I gave him all the slack I could, but the last two blunders were just too serious to be overlooked.'

'What are you talking about?'

'Allowing a fourteen-year-old multiple murderer to spend time alone with a three-year-old girl who has already been traumatized by a kidnap. That's bad enough. But then allowing that same murderer to walk away free afterwards, with two knives in his coat pockets. I think you'd have to agree that those are pretty catastrophic errors of judgement.'

I don't answer. I can't think.

Bannerman's finished. That's clear. Probably Fern too. But there was all the stuff I gave him. The information. And the backup drive. Hawk's external hard drive.

I see Jakes watching me. With that hidden smile again.

'Yes,' he murmurs. 'The information was very useful. Very useful indeed.'

And he turns, reaches back into the drawer, pulls something out. Drops it on the desk beside him. I recognize it right away. Haven't seen it for three years.

But it's like I buried it yesterday.

The backup drive from Hawk's computer.

Jakes stands up, smiles down at me. Then stretches up with the hammer and slams it back down again.

Into the drive.

It shatters in one go, pieces flying everywhere, but he goes on beating down with the hammer, a mad grin ripping over his face. Till there's nothing left of the drive.

Or my hopes.

He calms down, stands over me again, raises the hammer once more. I feel myself flinch, in spite of my efforts. He watches me, and a glare of satisfaction darkens his eyes.

Then without another word, he flings the hammer away and strides out of the room. For a few moments I hear his feet pounding the corridor, just like the other two porkers. Then the sound fades. I hear a motor start up, drive off. And silence falls again.

But not for long.

From the door behind comes a click. I twist round, stare towards it. It opens slow. And there's four gobbos standing there.

Darkness. A cold stone floor. And me lying on it. Can't see much more. But I know enough. I know I've been knocked out and drugged. I know I've been driven somewhere. I know who's got me. So I know it's the end.

Yeah, Bigeyes.

I won't come back from this.

I got pain slamming my head where they blammed me. Drowsy too but not much, cos they only drugged me a little. They want me awake, Bigeyes. Shit, they want me awake. If you haven't worked out why, you soon will.

Footsteps.

Bang, bang, bang.

I struggle up. Got to be standing. Got to look like I got some spit. Even if I haven't. Crunch of the door, flick of a switch. Light blasts into my face. Single light, straight above me.

I check round quick. Small room, no windows. Long table down the middle, chair close by. Brick walls, nothing on 'em but a blank screen at the far end. Four gobbos in the doorway.

The grinks who came to fetch me from Jakes. They don't waste time. Door clunks closed and they're on me straightaway. Nothing I can do. Except go inside myself. I can't beat 'em, can't escape.

They laugh, pick me up like I'm a doll, dump me on the chair, crowd round, leering. Big gobbos, beefbags, the worst kind of shit. I know what this is, Bigeyes. Oh, yeah. This is trophy time. And here's the man who's won. Right in front of the chair. Face in the screen.

Hawk.

Come to watch the fun.

And celebrate his triumph.

He's sitting in a small room. Somewhere cosy,

somewhere far away. Nice easy chair. He's got a casual shirt on, loose at the neck, and his hair's glossy, like it's just been washed. He sips a drink, pops an olive in his mouth. Sees my eye catch him.

Grins.

They push me off the chair, kick me over to the screen, haul me up, stuff my face against the glass. Inches away I see Hawk laughing. He sips his drink again, spears another olive. The gobbos yank me higher.

And there's his eyes, digging into mine like darts. He's going to speak in a moment, going to drip some gloaty words over me. But he doesn't. Just goes on laughing as they pull me away, dump me back on the chair.

I glare back at the face in the screen. I want to drop my head, screw my eyes closed, but I want to glare back too. I want to throw all the hate I got inside me for that smirking bastard. So I make myself glare back, glare back, glare back.

Till I see nothing more.

Cos everything's gone dark.

When I come to, I'm lying on the floor again. I'm

aching, shivering. Feel like I've been lying here some time. Don't know for sure. Can't remember what happened at the end. And I don't want to. I just know it's dark and I'm cold.

And it's not over. Oh, no. Bullet in the head? I wish. But it's not going to be like that. Hawk'll want much more than that before he kills me.

Yeah, Bigeyes. I said *he*.

This is personal. He'll let his grinks do the business, and he'll watch every moment, savour every second from his comfy chair. But the final bit. The kill.

He'll do that himself.

Don't ask me how I know.

I try to sit up. Hard to move. I'm aching all over, pain pounding. I keep breaking into tears. I stare about me. Same room. They haven't moved me. They've turned off the light again but I can see enough now.

Table, chair, screen—blank again, thank Christ.

And me, whimpering.

I make myself stand up. Floor's slippery with blood. Got to be mine. They must have knocked me about a bit at the end. I don't remember. Just remember the darkness. I reach up, feel my face.

Sticky round the nose and mouth.

I step over the blood, plod to the far corner of the room. Darker there and I want darkness right now. I slump down, huddle back against the wall, pull my knees into my chest.

Feel the tears come back.

I'm so scared, Bigeyes. Scared of death and even more scared of torture. And both those things are coming. Trust me. I know how this works. First the gloating. So I know he's got me. Then the wait. An hour, two hours, whatever. To make my mind do what it's doing now.

Spin pictures of what's going to happen.

And then they'll come back. And it'll start.

Hawk's won. He's got everything he wanted. Jakes working for him as his personal poodle. The computer backup drive destroyed. The gangster bojos'll give him some sludge, but they won't have enough to plug him.

Not on their own. It needed the porkers to do their bit, and now Bannerman's finished, that's over too. Specially with Jakes in charge. Like I say, Hawk's got everything. And now he's got me too. And he'll be loving that.

He'll squeeze my life out slow as he can.

And lick all the juice as it goes.

Then I hear it.

Click of the door. It's opening again and I can see a figure standing there. For a moment I think it's Hawk. But it's too early for that. He won't come for me till I'm right at the end. Too weak to move, too weak to beg.

This is someone else.

Just a shadow so far. Gobbo, yeah, but still a shadow. He's just standing there, peering in. Searching the darkness, for me surely. Maybe he can't see me yet. I keep still, try to think.

There's something familiar about this guy.

But I can't crack what it is.

And there's something else.

He's wary. He's looking for me, yeah, no question. Who else would he be looking for? But he's standing there on the edge, and he's got the door half-open. I'm sensing he's on his own. And I got a feeling he's not supposed to be here.

So it's private.

Whatever this is.

Now I got him. I recognize the shape. The neck, the head. He was in the car, Bigeyes. At the school, yeah? He was one of the minders looking after Damien. Not the driver. The other grink.

And now I'm guessing the rest.

I rammed their motor, remember? And the last thing I saw of those two was this gobbo chasing after me. And his mate slumped over the steering wheel. I might just have killed him. Which case this gobbo's here for some justice.

On behalf of his mate.

That could be bad.

But it might also be good. It might even be a chance. Cos I'm telling you, Bigeyes, whatever this guy's come for, he'll know he can't kill me. It'd be more than his slimy life's worth if he deprives Hawk of his kill. And he won't forget that for a second.

So he's taking a risk here. And he's got to watch his step.

Like I got to watch mine.

He's coming in. Seen me now, worked out where I am, safe in the corner. No chance of escape. He closes the door, locks it on the inside. Drops the key in his right pocket. I keep still, check him cute as I can.

Hard to tell if he's got a knife. He won't use one anyway. Too dangerous for him. Cos even if it doesn't kill me, it'll leave a mark. He'll use fists and feet. And hope the blood and bruises get mixed up with the rest.

He's walking over.

Slow.

I scramble up, struggle towards the chair. Only weapon in the room. But he cuts me off easy. Stands there, blocking my way, glowering. He's not here for fun, this gobbo. Not leering like Hawk. Or just carrying out orders like the four grinks.

This one's raging. And I know I'm right. It's for his mate.

He doesn't talk. Just comes for me.

Fast, low.

Plunges into me, rams me against the wall, flings me on the ground, falls on me. I feel my breath rasp out, and now I'm choking. He's got his hands tight round my throat and he's squeezing, squeezing.

I stare up into his face. His eyes are black blades and he's got spittle round his mouth. He tightens his grip. Jesus, Bigeyes. He's going for it. He's not going to hold back like I thought. He's saying stuff you, Hawk, I'm stiffing this bastard for myself.

Then I feel it, thank Christ. A hesitation in his hands, just a flash, like he's suddenly remembered. I stretch out, crunch his groin in my fist. He gives a roar, slams my hand away, yanks me to my feet, butts me in the face.

I stagger, head swimming. He grabs me by the collar, hurls me towards the other side of the room. I thump onto the floor, skid past the table, smack the chair on its side. Squirm back up, quick as I can, but I'm stunned, I'm struggling to see.

Gobbo's lumbering over.

I snap hold of the chair, whip it round in front of me. Won't do much good but it's all I got. Gobbo takes no notice of it, comes on. He's spitting hate now and he won't hold back again.

He breaks into a run, like he can't wait. I brace myself. He dips his shoulder, charges, skids on the patch of blood. Stays upright but he's off balance and

I won't get a better chance. I step to the side, swing the chair, smash his legs away.

He falls against the side of the table, grasps hold of it, half-standing. I crash the chair over his head. He gives a moan, tumbles to the ground. I slam the chair over him again. He rolls away, lurches back up.

Turns to face me again.

I grip the chair, edge round, keeping the table between us. He's got blood pouring from his mouth and nose, but his eyes are darker than ever. He seizes the table, jerks it out of the way, blunders towards me.

Then stops, swaying on his feet.

I stare at him. His eyes are misting up. So are mine but his are worse. I twist the chair, hold it so the legs are pointing at him, charge. None of 'em catch his face but they lock round it, cage him in, and now I'm driving him back, back, back.

Smash!

The glass screen shatters as his head plunges into it. He gives a bellow, flails his arms. His body's heaving and rolling under me, but I go on driving him back, into the screen, into the broken glass.

Then stop.

Stand back, wait.

Chair poised.

The gobbo writhes, groans. His head's stuck in the broken screen, shattered glass sprinkling his hair. He shudders, pulls himself clear, moaning as the shards rip into him. His eyes are drowning but he fixes me with 'em.

I grip the chair, aim, lunge.

He goes down.

And this time doesn't come up.

I stand over him, panting. He's not dead. He's still breathing, but he's out cold. I got to be quick. No telling how long he'll stay out. And the other grinks could turn up any moment.

I drop to my knees, run through his pockets.

Key to the door, mobile, fob for his car.

Stuff everything in my pocket, stand up, take a breath. I'm swaying bad and my head's like a fog. Body's hurting worse than ever and I got blood slopping off me again. Some of it's this bastard's.

He stirs, just a bit. I step back, check him. He's still again, but I got a feeling he's picking up. I limp over to the door, put my ear to it. No sounds outside. Got to risk it. Key in, turn, ease the door ajar.

Listen again.

Still nothing.

Check through the gap. Dark corridor, no lights, no figures. Bung a glance back in the room. Gobbo's still lying there, not moving. Step out into the corridor, close the door, lock it, check round.

Same as before. Silence, darkness, nobody in sight.

Corridor goes only one way. Set off down it, shuffling with the pain. Can't run. If they come for me, I'm dead. No way I can run. Not now. Been hurt too bad. I can hardly stand. Vision's going and I'm bumbling like a duff.

Don't let me lose it, Bigeyes.

If I keel over, I'm grilled. I got to stay upright, got to keep walking. And stay alert somehow. Cos Christ knows where I am and how many grinks I got to wig it from.

End of the corridor. It's turning left. Stop, check round the corner.

Another corridor, but it's short, and there's a small

door at the end. Down to it, panting like before, stop. Jesus, Bigeyes, don't let it be locked. Please don't let it be locked. Cos I can see straight off my key won't fit.

Shit, it's locked. And I can't pick this one. Wrong kind.

I lean against the door, gasping for breath, head spinning worse than ever. I try to think. I was sure I got everything out of that grink's pockets. But he wouldn't have slammed his way into this building if he couldn't get out again. So he must have brought a key for this door.

And either he hid it somewhere in the corridor to make double sure I can't get out. Or he's got it in another pocket and I missed it. So I got to go looking. Nothing else for it.

Cos there's no other way out. No window anywhere to crawl through. And no other door but this one. Hawk chose a good place for his filthy work. I start off down the corridor—then catch a sound.

Footsteps.

Scramble back to the door, put an ear to it.

Silence again. But I'm sure I heard something. For a moment I feel a chill of panic, like that gobbo's broken out of the room and he's coming for me. Then I catch the sound again, and it's steps, and they're not coming from down the corridor.

But from the other side of this door.

And they're heading towards it.

I dive to the side, just in time. Rattle of a key in the lock, then the door swings open. I crouch behind it, low as I can, fists clenched. All I got left now. Fists. Cos whoever's coming in's going to clap me the moment they turn to close the door.

And if it's more than one grink, I got no chance at all.

Got no chance anyway, even with one.

Door swings into me and there's a tramp of feet through the gap. Door starts to swing closed again. I get ready to fight.

But the tramping feet go on.

I crouch there, staring. It's the four grinks who worked me over before and they're striding down the corridor, none looking back. The last gobbo simply left the door to shut by itself.

It's already nearly closed.

I reach out, catch it before it locks, check the

gobbos again. They're turning into the long corridor but still in sight. I hold my breath, wait . . .

They disappear from view.

And I'm out the door.

Check round, quick, quick. They'll be out again any second, moment they see what's happened. And I'm getting groggier with every step. Blink round. Hard to see where I am. Darkness is falling and there's a storm blowing up.

Lane straight ahead, walls either side. Think it bends off to the right. Got to hit that point and get round it before the grinks burst out. Nowhere else to go. I blunder off, best I can. Head's clouding and I'm hurting like I want to scream.

Bend in the lane. Least I got this far. Check back. Place I was in looks like some kind of outhouse. No other buildings nearby. But I got no time to think of that. I'm desperate to find that grink's car. Just praying it's somewhere close, somewhere on its own.

But I don't suppose there's much chance of that.

I stumble on, up the next part of the lane. Dirt

track running off it to another outhouse, up on the rise. Van and three cars parked outside. I hobble towards 'em. Got to go for it, Bigeyes, got to take a risk. I stagger on, up the slope, up the slope, fast as I can go.

But it's horribly slow.

Storm's getting stronger and the wind's loud up here on the higher ground. But I still catch the slam of the door behind me, and the sound of footsteps charging after me. I limp on, closer, closer. Here's the second outhouse. Here are the motors. I stab the key fob at 'em. Car on the left flashes, unlocks.

Check behind.

No sign of the grinks yet but they won't be long. From inside the outhouse comes the sound of gobbos laughing. Jesus, Bigeyes. Don't let 'em rip out now. Open the car door, soft as I can, jump in, key in the ignition, check round.

Got to be something, got to be something. Rummage in the glove compartment—nothing. Lockers, doors, tray under the steering column—nothing. Under the driver's seat—gotcha.

Screwdriver.

I was hoping for a knife but this'll do.

Out of the car and now there's figures racing up the track. Same four grinks and they're bawling into the storm to their mates in the outhouse. I crash over to the van, plunge the screwdriver into the front tyre, over to the other motors, same again.

Back to the car, jump in, flick on the central locking.

Start the engine.

Figures swarming round now. The gobbos from the track and more grinks pouring out of the outhouse. Two jump on the bonnet, two more on the roof. I rev up, ease the clutch. The car brays and thunders forward.

Rain's pelting down now, hard, heavy drops, but still there's gobbos piling onto the car. Three on the bonnet, four, five. More throwing 'emselves on the roof. Car's moving but groaning under the weight.

I swerve, swerve again. Grinks tip off both sides. But some are still clinging on. I spin the wheel, left, right. More bodies fly off. Nobody left on the bonnet now. Don't know about the roof.

Check the mirror. Figures behind me, rolling on the

ground. Hard to tell if I got 'em all off the car. But I think so.

Thump!

A fist smacks into the side window. Glass doesn't shatter, but the fist tries again. I see the guy's face upside down, fuming in at me from the top of the car. Christ knows how he's hanging on. I speed up, race for the end of the track.

Slam the brake.

Car skids to a halt. A dark form torpedoes off the roof, bounces on the bonnet, rolls over the ground in front of the car. Gives a shudder, starts to stand up. But I'm moving again, foot down, speeding up, speeding up.

Gobbo turns, glowers at me.

'Yeah, grink,' I murmur. 'Stay there if you want.'

He jumps aside at the last minute.

And I scream past.

Down the lane, searching hard. I didn't see a way out before. Just the track heading up to the second outhouse. There's got to be another way out of wherever this is. Cos I'm telling you, Bigeyes. I got no idea where we are.

Snap on the headlights, full beam.

There's the first outhouse, where they kept me. And now I can see better. This lane bends round the building and off past it. Christ knows where it goes after that but I got no choice. Can't go back.

Bump past the outhouse, on down the lane. It's twisting and falling, dronky broken walls either side. No clue where this ends up. Just got to hope it takes us to a main road. And then we got to pelt.

Cos I'll tell you something, Bigeyes. This area's going to be flooded in minutes. Never mind me stuffing the tyres back there. That'll help but only a bit. There'll be backup cracking in here before you can blink.

If I don't break out in ten minutes, I won't break out at all.

Lane's still falling. Hilly little place, whatever this is. Don't recognize any of it. Touch of the country but not leafy green. Hard to see with the darkness and rain. And my head's not helping.

Eyes are blearing up again.

And my body's blamming.

I forgot about both in the gig back there, but now I'm loose, it's all come back. I got to grip hard, keep my spit, or I'll crash this motor right now. Shake my head, shake it again, peer out.

Wipers. Use the bloody wipers. See, Bigeyes? I'm not thinking right. Should have stuck 'em on first go. Feel round, find the wiper switch, flick 'em on.

Junction straight ahead.

Stop, check for a signpost.

Nothing.

Left, off down the road. Don't ask me why I turned this way. Got no idea. Foot down, squeal the motor. Least this baby can shift. Keep my eyes on the road and the lights digging through the cloud of rain. It's growing heavier all the time. Trees on both sides of the road now, bending with the wind.

Another junction. No sign like before.

Left again.

Just a hunch.

Or not even that. Just got to keep moving. Keep moving and hope.

Foot down again. Headlights coming the other way. I check 'em close. Could be anything. It's a lorry. I watch it cute, but it's straight past. More headlights, opposite side.

I keep going, keep watching. They all pass. I drive on, fast, fast. Hoping for another junction. I want to get off this road now. Been on it too long. And I want a signpost. I want to know where those bastards took me.

Garage on the left, police car by one of the pumps. No sign of anyone filling up. But there's two porkers in the station, talking to the girl on duty. I flash past. Check the mirror.

No one coming after me.

Drive on, faster still. Got to put all the distance I can between me and anyone else. And the road's clear for the moment so I'm hoping the speed won't attract attention. But I need another junction. I need it soon.

Roundabout, big one. And a huge great signboard to go with it.

OK, OK.

I got where we are now. They took me north of the Beast, Bigeyes. Right out to where the green country starts. Cute little place for a torture chamber, right? And Hawk'll have plenty more like that.

You better believe it.

Onto the roundabout, last exit, off down the road.

Yeah, Bigeyes, I know.

You're wondering why I'm heading back towards the Beast. You're thinking—you got away from the grinks and you got a nice fast car. So why not use it? Why not drive north, far as you can. Petrol gauge says full tank so why not use up all the juice, dump the motor, wig it further, go to ground? You might just live.

Yeah, Bigeyes. I might just live.

Only it won't work now. That kind of living. Cos there's something I've found out since I met Becky, and Mary, and Jaz, and Ruby, and Poppa, and even a few others. Like Bex and Bannerman.

I've found out there's things you can't ever run away from. Cos they just keep running with you. If you don't know what I'm talking about, tough. Cos I'm not explaining it. I just know I'm not running. I'm going back.

Cos there's one last thing to do.

If I can stay alive long enough. That's the smack-end of it. And I don't just mean grinks rubbing me out. I mean my body giving up. Cos I can feel my life dribbling out by itself.

They hurt me bad, those bastards. I'm struggling to see, struggling to stay upright. I want to slop over, close my eyes, fade away, not come back. But I can't let that happen. Not yet. Got to do this last thing.

It's sitting there in my head, fighting the darkness that's already there. But I can still see it, this thing. Cos it's got a darkness of its own. A bigger darkness. I just hope I can live long enough to slam it through. Only . . .

Shit!

Car's swerving off the road. Jerk the wheel, swing us back on course, check the mirror, breathe out. Breathe again. Bloody hell, Bigeyes. I lost it, lost focus. Still losing focus. See what I mean?

My eyes are fogging up again.

Got to pull over, rest, just a bit, get my head right. I need a lay-by, or better still, a quiet road, somewhere dark. No sign of anywhere yet, and the traffic's building up too. Both ways, specially coming up behind, heading for the Beast.

Christ!

I'm swerving again.

Blare of a horn behind me. I pull the car straight, hide my face, feel a car scream past. Another blare of the horn as it goes. Look back at the road. Jesus, Bigeyes, this is bad.

I got to rest. And soon.

Lay-by, just ahead. Don't like the look of it. Too exposed. But I got no choice. Another minute on the road and I'll crash. Slow down, easy, easy. Got to look like everything's cute. No waggling the car.

Indicate, brake, pull in. Take a breath, think. Handbrake up. Good boy. Lights off, wipers off. Kill the engine. Breathe.

Traffic roars past, thundering towards the Beast. I can't stay long, Bigeyes. Too risky. Any neb can see me parked here and grinks'll be ploughing up this road. Porkers too.

Just a couple of minutes. No more.

Can't sleep. Mustn't sleep.

Close my eyes.

Mustn't sleep.

But it falls over me like a shroud. A big, black shroud, deep and warm and good—till the nightmare starts.

And Christ, I'm back in that room. I didn't get away, and Hawk's still watching me, grinning, grinning. And it's not just him now but other nebs too. It's like a gallery of faces, each one in its own little glass screen. They're all round the room, staring out.

And it's not just grinks. It's people who shouldn't be watching. It's Becky and Jaz and Mary. And now other faces. Bannerman and Fern. Ruby, Poppa and all their mates. Trixi and the trolls. Dig and Riff. And more faces, nebs from the past. The people I killed.

And suddenly I get it, Bigeyes.

Everyone's watching. That's right. Everyone I've ever known, good or bad. They're all watching. I'm in the room and I can't get away and the grinks are starting to rip up my life, one piece at a time.

'Ah!'

I'm awake. I'm gripping the steering wheel, my body shaking, my head blasting like it wants to split open. I lean back, gaping with the pain. And catch a glint of headlights in the mirror.

Someone's pulling in to the lay-by.

I try to calm down, get my head straight. Don't

know who this is but I'm not waiting to find out. Start the engine, lights on, check mirror, pull out. Check mirror again. Other motor's stopped in the lay-by. Gobbo in a suit, naffing into a mobile.

Nobody with him.

But he's staring in my direction.

Might mean nothing. Speed up, check the mirror again. Other car's pulled out too, coming on fast but staying in my wake. Gobbo's still talking into his mobile. Catches me up, snaps in behind, puts his mobile down.

I go on watching him. He stays there for a bit, then starts to pull out. I whip my face the other way as he roars past. Check after him. He's blasting on now but I go on watching him till he disappears among the lights ahead.

I'm doing this all wrong, Bigeyes. Just shows I got my brain smashed. I never should have come this way. Too busy. That gobbo might be nothing, just some fancy dimp showing off his motor.

But I'm too big a target on this road.

Should have snagged off way back. Trouble is, I'm so weak and that's what fixed me on this road. I've only got so much spit left in me so I thought I better take the fastest route.

But maybe I'm zipping myself over. Cos if I'm honest with you, Bigeyes, I wasn't really thinking about the fastest route. Truth is—I just wasn't thinking. About anything.

So I better start now.

OK, got to wig it off this road. That's the first thing. Take the straggly way into the Beast. Never mind how weak I'm feeling. Got to take the safest route. Won't be much better than this road, but it might be a bit.

Rain's stopped. Wind's gone down.

Junction ahead.

I watch it, cute as I can. Cuts off round the north of the Beast, but there's roads off it I can use. Side roads, little lanes. Going to take a while to get in. But I got to crack that. However much I'm hurting.

Left, off the road.

Down to the roundabout, second exit, right at the motel, over the bridge, past the shops. Check the car clock. Six in the evening. Jesus, Bigeyes. Was I that long with those bastards? I lost all track of time. And now the night's coming back.

Switch on the radio. Got to hear this one.

'The news at six o'clock.'

And I feel my mouth drop open. Cos I'm the first item. It's all about me. My name, my life, stuff they've pieced together. The number of dronks I killed. How I ran away to the old city, played dead, made friends with Mary, ran off with Bex and Jaz. Came back to the Beast. How I'm dangerous, how I'm still at large. How I shouldn't be approached.

It's all in the bulletin.

Except one thing.

Lord Haffler-Devereaux.

No mention of him at all. Just stuff about me getting mixed up in the gangster underworld. But what did you expect? Jakes will have cherry-picked the bits he wanted from Bannerman's report.

The news goes on.

More violence, more arrests in the Beast. Only telling us so much. No names, like before. But I'm thinking names, Bigeyes. You bet. Names from the past, names I wrote down on those lists. Not just the bojos and gangster dregs but the city nebs, bankers, business bums and other spikes from Hawk's smoky world.

And the biggest name of all.

Lord Haffler-Devereaux.

I wish those names were on the news. Christ, I do.

The bulletin goes bumbling on. But I'm only half-listening now. I got the drift. The net's spreading wider and that's good. Yeah, Bigeyes, that's very good. Only problem is, it's nowhere near good enough.

Not to nail Hawk.

The gangster bojos won't get him on their own. Nor will the porkers. He'll stay safe from all the grime and sweep away every track that leads to him. He can sit cute in his nest, specially now he knows the backup drive from his computer's been slammed.

He'll be mad though. I'm telling you, Bigeyes. He might be safe but his world's crumbling around him and he'll be out of his mind with rage. And that's what I'm counting on. I need him to be mad.

For what I got planned.

OK, think. Stay awake, stay alive, and think.

Radio off, check the road. Two things I got to do quick and there's a place just round the corner that's cute for both. Long as it's not too crowded. And the payphone's still working.

Cos I don't want to use the grink's mobile. Not for this. Don't want him tracing the number I rang. Good news is I spotted something in the glove compartment earlier when I was looking for a blade to stab the tyres. Something I'm hoping I can use.

I'll show you later.

On down the road, round the corner.

There you go. Garage, phone box, burger kiosk. And only a few nebs hanging round. Pull in, drive over to the far side of the parking area, check round. No cars nearby. Lights off, engine off.

Check again.

Nobody looking, nobody coming over. Just a few cars parked here. Three nebs by the kiosk, nobody in the phone box. Reach over, open the glove compartment. There it is, Bigeyes.

A wallet.

Nice fat one too, so I'm hoping there's some decent jippy inside. And I'm going to need it. Cos I got to spend some money tonight. Right, let's see what the bastard had on him.

Jesus, this'll help. And all in crispy notes. Won't be enough though. I'm still going to have to crawl back into that tunnel I showed you. Remember it? The old snakehole where I stashed the money?

Going to need all of that.

And probably still have to barter.

Anyway, let's get on with it.

Stuff the notes in my pocket, poke about the wallet for some loose change. Yeah, plenty. Let's go. And hope our boy's in tonight.

Over to the phone box. Couple of faces check me out from the cars. Couple more from the kiosk. I keep my face dark in the hood. New car drives in, swishes into a parking space.

Flash motor.

Two gobbos in suits. They don't get out. Just sit there, talking.

Looking round.

I step into the phone box, check for a dialling tone. It's cute. Flick a glance round at the car park. Gobbos still sitting in the flash motor. Nobody looking my way. I got to do this. Whatever else is going on.

Coins, number, dial.

He better be in, Bigeyes. He better bloody be in.

Click of the phone. Sound of a television. And a radio. Then a voice.

'Yeah?'

'Hello, Ezi.'

He doesn't answer. I hurry on, before he kills the phone.

'It's Blade.'

'I worked that out.'

'I see Nelson's been busy.'

'Yeah, man. He got one big shopping list.'

'He must be pleased with you.'

'What's your point?'

Slam of a car door. I check the parking area. One of the suits has got out. Trigging over to the kiosk. Other gobbo's staying put. I go on.

'There's something I want you to get me.'

'Like what?'

I take a breath. I'm choked about this, Bigeyes. Choked out of my head. I'm weak and I'm hurt and I'm not thinking good, and I need Ezi to do this badly. He's the only neb I'll ever talk into getting me what I want.

'Like what?' he snaps.

I tell him, slow as I can, clear as I can. What I want, what it's for. He hears me through, then chuckles.

'Sure you want this?'

'Why not?'

'Don't sound like your kind of style, boy.'

'It's what I want,' I say. 'And you got no cause to complain. I told you what I want it for.'

'You sure did.'

'So it's going to end up helping you big time, right?'

'Oh, yeah.' Ezi chuckles again. 'It's gonna help us big time.'

I check the parking area again. Kiosk's almost cleared. The other nebs have gone back to their cars and it's just the gobbo in the suit getting served.

I take a breath. So far, so good.

But now it gets tougher.

'I need it tonight, Ezi.'

'Oh, is that so?' he gloats. 'Man in a hurry, right?'

'Can you do it? And how much will it cost?'

He doesn't chuckle this time. He laughs out loud.

'I can get that for you in two hours. And it ain't

gonna cost you nothing. No, sir. Considering what we gonna get when you done finished, you can have that baby for free. With Mr Nelson's blessings on top.'

He laughs again, a long, mocking laugh.

Don't like the way this is going, Bigeyes. I know Ezi can get me what I want and I expected him to chew me up a bit before he agreed. What's bothering me is—will he deliver?

I didn't expect a freebie. I thought I'd have to pay. I almost want to pay. Cos that way I got a chance of him turning up with something. Even if I have to fight him for it. But if he's just having fun, I could get nothing. Or worse still, turn up and get spiked.

But I guess I got no choice.

'OK,' I start, 'I'll meet you at—'

'No, no,' he cuts in. 'You don't tell me where to meet. I tell you. You got that?'

I frown. I knew he'd bomb me on this. I don't like it, Bigeyes. It could be more than him having fun. He might be setting me up for another gig with him and Spit. And this time they'll come prepared.

'I'm not coming to your flat,' I say.

'I don't want you in my flat. You been there once already and I don't want your smell back.' He pauses. 'End of my estate there's a park with a playing field. You know it?'

'Yeah.'

'Bottom of that there's some trees.'

'I know 'em.'

Shit place to meet, Bigeyes. For me anyway. Cute enough for Ezi if he's planning to jump me with Spit and their mates. Cos they got a hundred places to hide among all those shadows.

'Meet me there in two hours,' he says.

And hangs up.

Can't say I'm surprised, Bigeyes. I kind of expected this. Or something like it. But I guess that's how things are now. All or nothing. I step out of the phone box, dip my head further inside the hood, trig over to the kiosk.

Nobody there now, just the gobbo behind the counter. Smell of burgers and onions cooking. I wander up, face low. Gobbo chirps out at me.

'What can I do for you, mate?'

'Two burgers, two lots of chips, two cans of Coke.'

'Onions?'

'Yeah, thanks.'

I catch him bung a look round the car park. Don't know if he saw me turn up on my own in the grink's car. I'm hoping not cos if he did, he'll be wondering about my age.

With any luck he just thinks I'm ordering for two and some other neb's driving the car I came in. But he goes on looking round the car park. I got to stop him doing that.

'Can I have some ketchup with it?'

He looks back at me.

'Some ketchup?' I say. 'Please.'

He sniffs, fixes the food. I half-turn, wait.

'There you go,' he mutters.

I give him the money, take the food, wander off towards the garage. Got to head this way for a bit, make him think I'm nothing to do with that motor at the other end of the car park.

I walk a bit further, check round, cut right, out of his sight-line, trig back behind the kiosk, round it to the car. Stop, check round.

Nobody watching me from the other motors, far as I can tell. And someone else has stepped up to the kiosk and the gobbo behind the counter's turned to fix more food.

Slip into the car, hood down, start up. Drive off, keeping to the edge of the car park. Turn my face away from the kiosk and the other motors. Don't know if anyone's worked me out. But there's nothing I can do about that now.

Back on the road, down to the lights, straight over, left at the junction. Gobbling the burgers as I go. Jesus, they taste good. Two lots? I wish I'd bought three. I didn't just buy two so I could spin that gobbo's head. I bought 'em cos I'm starving.

The chips go the same way as the burgers.

So does the Coke.

Drive on, watching, watching.

Getting close now, Bigeyes. And I'm choking again. I hate this estate. Worried about the time too. Two hours, Ezi said. That would have been no bum gripe if it hadn't been for the gobbo in the kiosk. I wasted precious minutes stinging that dimp.

Round the roundabout, past the cinema, left at the lights.

And there it is, down at the bottom of the hill.

Recognize that? Block of flats where Ezi hangs out. Only last time we came, we hit it from the other side. I'm keeping away from that end, Bigeyes.

You know why?

Cos we're not crossing the playing field to get to the trees. That way they can hide and watch me coming. We'll park over there on the right and I'll climb the fence into the trees and come at 'em from the other direction. That way I might get a chance to check who's there before I show myself.

Just hope I got enough strength to scrape over that fence.

Check round, wait for a gap in the traffic, pull over. Check again. Nobody on the pavement. Engine off, lights off. Wait. Check over the road.

There's the fence, see? And the trees on the other side. You can just get a glimpse of the playing field beyond. Glance at the car clock.

Dead on time.

So they should be there.

Yeah, Bigeyes. It won't just be Ezi.

Out of the car. Don't slam the door. Close it soft. Over the road, quiet, slow. Eyeshine over the fence.

Think I can climb that. Hang on, I don't need to. I can squeeze through that gap down there.

Creep over, scrape through.

Grass under my feet and hard bony roots. Stop at the first tree, peer round. No sign of Ezi or anyone else. Just shadowy trunks reaching up to the sky. I take a step forward, another, another. Then hear a voice growl behind me.

'Get the bastard!'

I whirl round, brace myself—and see Ezi standing there. He's slipped between me and the fence and he's blocking my way back to the street. No sign of him carrying what I came for. But he'll be carrying something.

A gun probably.

I check round me. No sign of any other nebs.

Look back at Ezi.

And see him laughing. He doesn't speak, just goes on mocking, like he did on the phone. I go on checking round. He could still have slugs backing him up. Spit's bound to be here somewhere.

Ezi catches my thought.

'He ain't here, man.'

I check again. Ezi shakes his head.

'Spit ain't here. Nobody ain't here. Just you and me.'

I still don't believe him. And why hasn't he got the stuff I asked for? He catches that thought too.

'It's over there.' He nods into the trees. 'Didn't feel like carrying it to the fence.'

'What did you come over here for anyway?'

'Cos I guessed you'd climb over. Wouldn't risk crossing the field. Too easy to spot. So I thought I'd give you a surprise.'

Ezi starts laughing again.

'You see? Not that clever, are you?'

He stops suddenly, fixes me.

'You're hurt, man.'

I shrug.

'Let's get on with it.'

He takes no notice, steps over, peers into my face.

'You hurt bad. Who done that?'

I don't answer. Ezi goes on staring at me. And there's something in his face, Bigeyes. Something I'd never have expected. Not friendship. Jesus, no. But I'll tell you one thing. He's stopped laughing at me.

But I don't like him watching me like this.

'I'm in a hurry, Ezi,' I mutter.

He straightens up, still watching me close.

'Is that so? Well, let's get moving.'

He turns, leads me into the trees, stops just before the playing field opens up.

'There,' he says.

Points to a lumpy bag resting on a stump. Bends down, picks it up.

'You got everything I asked for?' I say.

'See for yourself.'

He holds out the bag. I take it, poke about inside. It's all there. Even the extra bits.

'All ready to go,' says Ezi. He pauses. 'Sure you still want this?'

'Yeah.'

'It's mean shit.'

'Yeah, yeah.'

'I'll show you how it works,' he goes.

He doesn't need to. I can see how it works. But I let him tell me. He runs through it, thorough. Shows me twice. I feel myself fidget. I just want him to go. So I can go. And get this thing done.

'Piece of piss,' I say.

He looks up at me.

'Oh, it ain't hard. Ain't hard at all. Even a kid could handle it. And you ain't no kid.'

I stare back at him. Can't read his voice, Bigeyes. Or his face. Is he mocking me again? And why'm I bothered if he is? I shouldn't give two bells. But I do. For some reason. I hear myself speak. And suddenly I sound so young.

'I'm fourteen, Ezi.'

Why did I say that, Bigeyes? Eh? To this dronk, of all people. It just came out, like I couldn't stop it. There's a silence, a long silence. Ezi looks back at me, quizzical, then gives a slow smile.

'You ain't fourteen,' he says.

Leans close, whispers.

'You's as old as sin, brother.'

And he turns and walks off over the field.

I watch him go. He's trigging slow, steady, taking his time. Doesn't look back once. Weird, Bigeyes. I almost want him to. But he goes on walking, step

step step, a moving shadow, getting fainter all the time.

And then he's gone.

I'm shaking again. Pain's banging my head, my body. I open the bag, look inside. Feel the pain go on. Close the bag, clench my fists, turn, limp back to the fence.

Got to do this.

Nothing else left.

Whatever Becky thinks, and Mary, and Jaz, and Ruby, and Poppa, and Christ knows who else. Cos I'm telling you, Bigeyes, they're all shouting no. I can hear 'em right now, among the swaying trees.

No, no, no.

That's what they're saying.

And I'm saying—it's got to be this way.

Through the gap in the fence, back to the street, check round. Traffic moving, both ways. Smellies, taxis, motors. Picking up too. Got to watch myself, specially with this bag. Got to clap everything that moves, before it hits.

Wait for a gap, check faces, over the road, back to the motor. Jump in, check again. Nobody stopping, nobody ripping over. Bag on my lap. Feels strange lumped there. Can't drive like this, but I want it near me.

I know it's a risk, if I get stopped.

But I want it near me. Not in the boot. Push it over the passenger seat, down onto the floor, straighten up again. Take a breath. Take another. Check the petrol gauge. Still plenty. Enough for what I need anyway.

Whip a glance at the car clock.

Half past eight. Let's go.

Start up, check round, wait for a spot, pull out. Down to the bottom of the road, round the round-about, back the way we came. Yeah, Bigeyes, now you're wondering. Why are we heading north again?

Never mind. I'm too tired to explain. And I got too much to think about. And watch for. The roads are going to be worse now I got away from Hawk. Every grink'll be out, and every porker too. The good porkers and the dodgy ones.

But you know what's strange? I've almost stopped worrying. Don't know why. I should be worrying. I will be later. Before dawn certainly. I'll be choked out of my head by then.

But right now, when there's most eyes watching for me, I'm just cute about driving. Sitting here driving, sweet on the speed limit, nice and legal. Steady steady. Like the way Ezi walked out of my life.

And here's something I hadn't expected. About driving steady. It's good for thinking. I told you just now I got lots to think about. Well, I have. But there's a second strange thing. About driving steady, I mean.

I'm getting a different kind of thinking.

I was going to think about what I got to do.

What's coming up.

But all I can think about is how beautiful the night looks. Yeah, Bigeyes, even here, cracking through the Beast. The lights of the shops, pubs, houses. The lights of the motors. The black sky reaching over us. And me, here, in this little moving snug. I've almost forgotten it's a grink's motor.

Cos it's not now.

It's mine. My little motor. My little moving snug.

Drive on, north, north, and now we're cutting west. Yeah, Bigeyes, heading right out to the edges of the Beast. Not where those bastards took me for their bit of sport. We're cutting west of that, and slamming further.

Out of the Beast altogether.

On, on, time ticking and my thoughts ticking with it. One hour, two, three, and still on. Check around you, Bigeyes. See how the roads have changed? The Beast has faded away and his energy's faded too. He's still there, heaving behind us, but cop this instead.

Main roads have gone and we're on a country lane. You're wondering how I know my way. Tough. Keep wondering. You should know me by now anyway. How I remember stuff.

Junction at the end. Right at the church, through the village, out the other side. Yeah, Bigeyes. We're not stopping here. We got a bit further to drive. And then a long walk after that.

On, on, climbing now, up the straggly lane. It narrows here. I remember it so well. There you go. Just hope we don't meet someone coming the other way. But we should be cute this time of night. And there's never much moving round here.

Look over at the bag in front of the passenger seat.

First time I've glanced at it since I dumped it there.

Not quite sure why.

I take my eyes off it, check the lane ahead. Still climbing, see? And then it dips off to the right. Top of the hill, stop, handbrake on. Keep the engine running. Lean back in the seat.

I'm breathing fast, Bigeyes. Too fast. But I can't stop myself.

Turn off the engine. Feel the silence fall over me. But I can still hear my breathing. I hate the sound of it. Kind of scares me. Reach out, turn on the radio.

More news. And it's the same again. Violence, arrests. My name in the bulletin. No mention of Lord Haffler-Devereaux. And there won't be. Trust me, Bigeyes.

They won't get him.

Radio off, take a breath. Climb out of the car. Feel the silence again. Funny how the storm died away so quick. Even if there's another one coming soon. I stand there, stare round.

Lane rolls away to the right, falling into the valley below. To the left, a track running down the side of the field, and right at the bottom, a lake glistening in the night, moonlight dancing on the surface.

So beautiful, Bigeyes. And you know what? I've been picturing that lake. No kidding. I remember it so well. I used to dream about it when I was sleeping rough in the old city.

A good memory, among so many bad ones.

Back in the car, engine on. Leave the lights off. Reach for the bag, rest it on my lap.

Drive.

Not down the lane. We're heading left, onto the track, down past the field, bump, bump, bump, car speeding up. Touch of the brake, just a bit. Not too fast, not yet. Bump, bump, bump. Track's getting rough. I'm starting to struggle with the wheel. But I got to hold it, got to keep us moving, and now I need more speed.

Touch of gas.

Bit more.

Faster, faster. Flash of moonlight, flash of bright water, rushing in, closer, closer, closer. One hand off the wheel, grab the bag, pull it tight. Open the door, fling it open. Bashes into a fence post, slams back at me. Kick it open again, check the track, the water, the rushing light.

Dive.

Out of the car, clutching the bag. I hit the ground, scream with the pain, roll over the track, spinning, spinning. And then I'm still. I hear the crash, feel the drops of shattered water rain upon me.

As the car plunges into the lake.

And disappears from view.

I stand up, stare down at the surface of the water. Already it's smoothing over, all traces of disturbance gone. Like the car never crashed in, like it never existed. And now everything's still again, just like it was.

Not a ripple

Just moonlight on water.

Oh, Jesus. If only I could do that with my life. Take everything that was ever bad and sink it, like I just sank that motor. Dump it in a lake, all gone in seconds, and then everything all right again.

Everything still.

Just peace and beauty.

And moonlight.

Only it doesn't work that way, does it? Not even with the car. You can sink it in a lake, hide it from view, but it's still there, isn't it? Even if no one ever finds it, you'll know it's there. It'll still exist.

But someone will find it.

Someone'll find everything you want to hide.

Cos you know what, Bigeyes? There's no secrets. Not really. I wanted to cut loose. From the knife, from the bad stuff I've done, from the past. But all I was trying to do was bury that shit. And that never works.

There's only one way to cut loose.

Really cut loose.

And this is it.

An owl calls, somewhere above me. I look back up the track. All quiet again, all still. But somewhere in the dark a bird's hunting. And now I got to go hunting too. Clasp the bag, hold it tight.

Set off up the track. Going to be hard work, even this bit up to the lane at the top of the hill. Don't ask me how I'm going to make it all the way, cos my body's hurting worse than ever. Panting already and I'm not even halfway up the slope.

Stop, take a few breaths, climb on, back to the lane, stop again. Bend over, gasp, straighten up. This could all go wrong, Bigeyes. I could hang about here for ever and still get zippo. I'm gambling the whole stack on one thing.

Hawk's anger.

I know he's mad. Oh, yeah, you bet. Question is— will he do what I think? If he does, then I got a chance. But it's all on this one throw.

Plod down the lane, into the valley. Got to stay smart, watch cute, however much I'm hurting. Going to be hooked on this road for a bit, so if a motor comes along, I'll have to hide. Getting spotted now could sting everything.

Walk, walk.

Makes me think back to the old city, Bigeyes. Remember how I used to like walking there? I told you about it once. How it straightens my head sometimes. Funny thing is, right now, here I am walking but I don't feel I got to straighten my head. Not any more. I reckon my head's pretty well sorted.

I'm getting scared, yeah. Course I am. Scared of what's coming. Like I told you, by dawn I'm going to be choking. But that's talking heart-wise. Head-wise I feel kind of clear. Like stuff's fixed itself. Maybe it's just knowing there's nothing else to do now.

No more decisions to make.

Cos in the end, Bigeyes, it's all very simple.

You do what you got to do. It's almost like the old days. When I was given some target. I did what I had to do. No questions asked. Wait, move in, hit hard. Hit again. Only difference is, what I did then was wrong.

What I'm doing now is right.

Walk, walk.

On down the lane, on through the night.

Keep thinking of that grink's mobile in my pocket. And all the people I wish I could speak to. I don't want to use it. Don't want those grinky bastards to ever know who I rang. Pull it out, check it over.

Gone dead anyway.

What the hell was I carrying it for? Stare down at it. Wipes me out suddenly looking at it. Maybe I should have used it, taken a chance. Could have spoken while I was driving here. Might have got through to Bannerman, Ruby.

Found out what happened to 'em. And Bex.

Maybe even got through to Mary.

But I guess I'm not meant to.

I fling the phone away, go on walking. Hear the owl call again. Getting colder. I try to brisk up, put on speed, but it's hard. I'm limping so bad. Peer up at the sky. Moon's still bright, and there's stars popping out like jewels.

Lane's twisting to the left, and starting to rise again. Still no motors cutting past. All's quiet like before, just the pad of my feet as I shuffle on. Something moves over to the right, something gliding.

The owl maybe.

But it's gone.

Climb, climb. This hill's higher than the last, but it gets better after that. And worse. Cos that's when we're close to the gig. Push on, clutching the bag, panting, panting. Brow of the hill seems like it's fixed, never drawing closer.

But slowly I'm getting there, up, up, just a small distance now. Here's the top. Low stone wall this side of the lane. Stop, slump on it, breathing hard. And then check down into the next valley.

There it is, Bigeyes.

See it? Straight ahead. Don't follow the lane. It ends up where we're going but waggles off a bit first. We're not trigging that way. We're cutting off here and heading straight down the side of the valley. So forget about the lane.

Check straight ahead.

In the distance.

Surrounded by trees.

The house.

Yeah, I know. You're thinking not that big. You were expecting a mansion, right? Well, it's bigger than it looks from here, but you're right. It's not a mansion. Tell you why.

It's a retreat, a secret den, a hideaway.

A nest.

Almost no one in the world knows Hawk owns this place. Not even his family. He told me that himself. And he hardly ever comes here. Once or twice a year maybe. And then only for a special reason.

I was that special reason once.

But I didn't come here with him. That's not how it worked. I was brought here separate, by car, by one of the few grinks allowed to know about Hawk's nest. Hawk's got his own way of getting here. And I won't know till we're closer if he's turned up tonight.

Come on.

Over the stone wall, scramble down the slope, down along the valley. I'm walking faster. Don't know where the strength is coming from, but suddenly it's like I can't wait to get there. Heart's pumping too. But it's not the excitement.

It's the fear I told you about.

The house is getting closer. I can see the trees clear, see the lane bending back in from the right. Tramping through a field now, sheep munching grass all around. Look up at me with moony faces, go back to their feeding.

I trudge on.

Trees draw closer, closer. They're blocking out most of the house from this level but I can see the shadow of it beyond. No lights, far as I can tell. This could all come to nothing, Bigeyes. Into the trees, stop, catch my breath.

The bag feels so heavy now.

Like I'm carrying my whole life.

Stumble through the trees, up to the edge of the fence. Peer over at the house.

All dark. No cars outside. Nothing. Like the place is locked up for the winter. I slump against the fence, back to the house. I was wrong, Bigeyes. I screwed up. I slammed everything on one throw. And the throw came to nothing.

Then I catch it, far off.

A low drone.

I stiffen. The sound grows louder, louder. I stare up and through the treetops clap the grey form slipping through the night, over the trees, over the house. I twist round, peer over the fence. And there it is, hovering in the dark.

Hawk's copter.

And now it's coming down.

I crawl back into the trees, find the blackest spot, close up on the ground, bag tight to my chest. I can't bear to look. And it's too risky anyway. Got to just listen. I hear the whirr of the engine, the swish of the blades, then silence. No doors banging, no voices, no footsteps on the gravel.

I start to shake. He won't be alone, Bigeyes. He can

fly the copter by himself but he won't be alone. He'll be protected like he always is, even in this secret place. Specially in this secret place.

I clench my fists, creep back to the fence, make myself check over.

Nobody in the copter. Lights on in the house.

And still silence.

Deep, cold silence.

Back into the trees, slump down again, stare at the bag. Feel the fear start to grow. Peer up at the sky again. I can still see the stars, Bigeyes, and the moon. And now something else.

The first streaks of light. Dawn's coming. Yeah, that's right. Another dawn I don't deserve to see. But neither does the bastard in that house. I take a long slow breath. Feel my mind clear, settle, harden. OK, Bigeyes, let's do it.

Revenge isn't sweet.

It's just necessary.

Tim Bowler is one of the UK's most compelling and original writers for teenagers. He was born in Leigh-on-Sea in Essex and after studying Swedish at university, he worked in forestry, the timber trade, teaching and translating before becoming a full-time writer. He lives with his wife in a small village in Devon and his work-room is an old stone outhouse known to friends as 'Tim's Bolthole'.

Tim has written nine novels and won thirteen awards, including the prestigious Carnegie Medal for *River Boy*. His most recent novel is the gripping *Bloodchild* and his provocative new *BLADE* series is already being hailed as a groundbreaking work of fiction. He has been described by the *Sunday Telegraph* as 'the master of the psychological thriller' and by the *Independent* as 'one of the truly individual voices in British teenage fiction'.

tim bowler

RISKING ALL

In the final instalment of Blade . . .

Dawn sky, dead sky. Deep, dronky grey. Clouds, no sun. Just the dream of it, somewhere far away. But you know what, Bigeyes? I never seen a dawn so beautiful.

There's something he aches for, Bigeyes. And it's constant. And when things are bad, that's when he craves it most. When he's choking with anger, like he is now, that's when he's got to have it. So he comes here. To make sure he can have what he wants. In secret.

Once upon a time, I was that secret.

Now we got more trouble. Motors turning up, three of 'em, flash-looking slammers. Fourth motor further off, purring up the lane. They pull in, nose round Hawk's copter, stop. Clunk of doors and more beef gets out. I'm counting fifteen.

Feel the stillness again. And the fear. Bend down, coil up the rope, rest it back on the ground. Pick up the bag, open it, look inside. It's all in here, Bigeyes. Everything I need now. My past, my present, my future.

Look up, Bigeyes. What do you see? The wall of the house, climbing, all the way to something you never spotted first time round. And you won't see it now cos of the mist and the dark. But it's there. A little tower at the top of the building. All on its own, built special. A nest, Bigeyes. A sanctuary for a dangerous man.

Let's go get him.